Praise for Natasha Moore's
The Ride of Her Life

"Ms. Moore has penned a great story of finding love and romance when you least expect it with a person you could spend the rest of your life with..."

~ *Sheryl, ecataromance*

"The Ride Of Her Life has a nice balance of heartfelt moments and scenes of careless exuberance of falling love. I'm actually quite sorry to see it end so soon."

~ *Mrs Giggles*

Recommended Read "The secrets in this story drew me into it and held my attention to the very end...Make sure you read The Ride of Her Life..."

~ *Missy , Fallen Angels Review*

"Natasha Moore has written a story that will leave you alternately crying and laughing as you turn the pages... This is definitely a keeper and a recommended read."

~ *Nickie Langdon, Romance Junkies*

D0911314

Look for these titles by
Natasha Moore

Now Available

The Passion-Minded Professor

The Ride of Her Life

Natasha Moore

A SAMHAIN PUBLISHING, LTD. publication.

Samhain Publishing, Ltd.
577 Mulberry Street, Suite 1520
Macon, GA 31201
www.samhainpublishing.com

The Ride of Her Life
Copyright © 2008 by Natasha Moore
Print ISBN: 978-1-59998-967-9
Digital ISBN: 1-59998-613-2

Editing by Laurie Rauch
Cover by Scott Carpenter

First Samhain Publishing, Ltd. electronic publication: November 2007
First Samhain Publishing, Ltd. print publication: September 2008

Dedication

To Rhonda, who helped me so much on this story and became a good friend in the process.

To Juliet, for the perfect title.

To the man in my life, you truly are my inspiration.

Chapter One

The day Dean Bastian walked into the bank was the day Sarah decided she was no longer going to be sensible.

But, to be honest, when it came to Dean, she'd never had a bit of sense. Seeing him again after all these years sent her right back to that gawky teenager who'd had a major crush on the bad boy next door.

Dean looked the same as she remembered, tall and dark in his black T-shirt and faded jeans. He crossed the lobby, his long legs covering the distance quickly. When she saw he was headed for her window, an unwanted thrill rippled across her skin. Her heart started beating faster and annoyance fought its way to the surface. She hated not being in control of her feelings.

There was enough she didn't have control of these days. Like doctors and hospitals and test results.

He set his motorcycle helmet on the counter in front of him and flashed a cocky smile that turned her knees to jelly. Oh, great, she was going to melt into a puddle of goo right in front of him. His dark blue eyes were laced with mockery as he slowly ran his gaze over her.

"Sarah Austin, still sitting in your little cage, I see."

She couldn't stop from blushing, but she wanted to cringe as the heat spread up her neck and across her face. She gritted her teeth at the jibe and struggled to get back in control.

"Hello, Dean," she said, working hard to keep her smile in place. "I understand you're skipping town again."

"Heading out on the Harley in the morning."

The little jab of envy didn't help her mood at all. What she wouldn't give to be going somewhere, anywhere but where her life was headed right now.

Then she remembered why he was in Buffalo to begin with and regretted taking her bad mood out on him. "I'm real sorry about your dad."

Dean nodded, the diamond stud in his ear winking at her. The cocky smile disappeared and his eyes shut down. She almost wished he was still teasing her. He didn't say anything, but Sarah wasn't surprised. She knew he and his father hadn't gotten along.

"Is Terry still in town?" she asked.

"She flew back to Denver yesterday." His face didn't tell her anything. She hoped he and his sister had settled their differences.

"She stopped in the bank for a minute the other day and I saw some pictures of her family. Her boys are cute."

"Yeah, they are."

"She works in a doctor's office?"

"Yeah."

Sarah was running out of small talk. For two people who'd grown up in the same neighborhood, on the same street for goodness sake, they couldn't have been more different. The annoying heart pounding didn't help any. And neither did the sweaty palms she rubbed on her skirt. Twenty-six was too old to still suffer from hopeless crush symptoms.

She pushed away an old memory of him wiping away her

tears. "What can I do for you this morning?"

He picked up the helmet and smoothly tucked it under his arm. "I need to sign a few more papers before I leave. Is Harry Larson busy?"

"I'll check." She picked up the interoffice telephone and called Harry, who told her to send Dean over. She pointed to the open office door across the lobby. "Go right in."

He looked her over once more. Ripples of hot awareness followed his gaze and she prayed she wouldn't blush again. "Good to see you, Sarah," he said softly, then turned and walked away.

She watched him go with a sense of relief. Sarah knew exactly why he bothered her. It wasn't the dangerous way he looked. He had always been sexy in a rough sort of way. She didn't even mind the dark hair that fell past his shoulders. It went with that rebel look he projected so well and most likely contributed to that crush she had. Correction, *used to have.*

No, what aggravated her was more what Dean represented. Freedom she had never known. Never would know.

"I'm glad he's gone," Jennifer, the teller next to her, said in a low voice. "He always scares me."

"Don't let him frighten you," Sarah said. "He's really not a bad guy."

Jennifer didn't look convinced. "Yeah, right."

Sarah had never been scared of Dean. He had fueled her teenage dreams and proved he could set her heart pounding even now. Still, she could understand Jennifer's reaction. Dean had always been the kind of guy mothers warned their daughters about.

Sarah could see Dean through the open doorway to Harry's office. He was perched on the edge of the seat, poised to escape at the first opportunity. Dean Bastian would never get caught in a cage.

Sarah sighed. "Can you believe people actually live like that?"

"Like what?" Jennifer asked.

Sarah nodded in Dean's direction. "I guarantee you that's one person who isn't tied down to a desk, doing the same old thing day after day. He doesn't let life just sweep him along. He probably has experiences. And adventures." Sarah leaned against her cash drawer. "What I wouldn't give for an adventure."

"Come on, Sarah. Get real. We're not kids anymore."

"But I never had any adventures," Sarah said softly, the emptiness of her life overwhelming her.

"I heard he's going back to L.A.," Jennifer said. "He's joining back up with the road crew for Aerosmith, if you can believe my oldest son."

Sarah nodded. Dean had been all over the country, all over the world probably. What was it like to see new places? To wake up to new sights and new people every day of the week? "He told me he was leaving tomorrow."

"There you go," Jennifer said. "Good riddance, I say."

Sarah didn't say anything. She stared at Dean, at the motorcycle helmet sitting on his knee. She shook her hands, trying to get rid of the pins and needles feeling that never really went away.

"Are you okay?" Jennifer asked.

Would she ever be okay again?

Since her last doctor's appointment, Sarah had started to look at life differently. Suddenly what had seemed important didn't matter much anymore. She just wasn't ready to talk about it yet. She didn't even want to think about it.

Sarah nodded at Jennifer. "I'm fine. My car died today." It wasn't the real reason for her distress, but true all the same. Her ancient, sensible Escort gave up the ghost in her driveway this morning. Now, on top of everything else, she had to shop for a new car before she could even think about going anywhere.

But as Sarah continued to look at Dean, a plan began to form in her mind. It was a crazy plan, definitely not sensible at all. But one that gave her hope where there had been none a few minutes ago. Before she could give herself time to change her mind, Sarah locked up her drawer and strode into the manager's office.

She wasn't going to let life cheat her out of her chance for adventure.

Dean couldn't relax when he got back from the bank. He crossed the dreary living room of the house he grew up in, went down the empty hallway, into the cheerless kitchen. The scarred furniture still took up space, the pictures of him and Terry when they were kids hung on the walls as they always had. But the people were gone. It wasn't home anymore.

Hell, it hadn't been home in a whole lot of years.

He opened the refrigerator and took out the six-pack of root beer from the otherwise empty interior. He was glad to be getting out of here. He hoped the house sold quickly. Too many memories, good and bad, were wrapped up in it.

Like the first time he rode his bike down the driveway. And the first time his dad threw him down the stairs.

13

Yeah, Dean was more than ready to leave this place behind.

As he wandered restlessly around the house, he could still see his mother sitting in the rocker by the good light before the cancer took her, knitting another sweater none of them wanted to wear. He and Terry always pleaded for stylish clothes like the other kids wore, but their father would grumble that they were ungrateful and tell them he wasn't going to spend good money on something their mother could make them for almost nothing.

Dean dropped onto the lumpy sofa and opened a bottle. Why did a trip home instantly throw you back to where you'd been before? Suddenly he felt like that rebellious kid he used to be, ready to take on the world all by himself and scared to death at the same time.

He had a good life now in Denver and a job he loved. Things were going okay. Better than he'd ever hoped. He hadn't turned out like his father, no matter what the old man had always said.

Dean jumped up from the sofa and paced around the house again, unable to sit still. Memories of the past kept tangling up with his thoughts of the future. Where did he go from here? Or rather, when he got back to Denver? What did he do with the rest of his life? He'd been feeling more and more restless lately and this trip down memory lane wasn't helping.

He'd finished the second bottle when he heard a knock at the door. Probably another one of the neighbors offering their condolences. He sighed and opened the door.

Sarah Austin stood before him. He'd forgotten how short she was, probably only about five-foot-one or so to his six feet. Her blonde hair was shiny and smooth and fell to her shoulders. Dean remembered when it used to hang to her waist in braids. She hid whatever shape she now had under a baggy denim jumper.

He could still picture her as a skinny kid trying to fight off the bullies in their neighborhood who liked to pick on the small and brainy. Somehow it had fallen upon Dean to be her protector. He'd pretended it annoyed the hell out of him, but in truth, he had never minded. Something about Sarah had always made him want to be there for her.

He couldn't quite decipher the expression on her face at the moment. Determination, maybe, and that made him a little uneasy. But she looked nervous too. He wasn't sure how that made him feel.

Come to think of it, he was never quite sure how he felt around Sarah.

"Hello again," he said. "Late lunch hour?"

"Um, not exactly." She looked up at him, chewing on her bottom lip. He'd forgotten how big her brown eyes were. "I need to talk to you."

He didn't like the sound of it already. "Okay. Do you want to come in?"

Sarah nodded, and took a deep breath, as if she had to work herself up to walk through the door. Or maybe it was talking to him that she had to build up the courage for. Whatever it was, she followed him into the living room.

He picked up one of the brown bottles of root beer sitting on the coffee table. "Thirsty?"

"No, thanks," she said quickly. Then she frowned and held out her hand. "I mean, sure. Thanks."

She stood there in the middle of the living room looking like she had no idea what she was doing there. She didn't say anything right away. She twisted the cap off the bottle and took a tentative taste. She looked up at him with surprise, obviously

15

expecting beer instead of soda.

He didn't tell her he'd had enough of the real thing back when he was young and stupid. When he'd finally had one too many hangovers and realized he would fulfill his father's prediction if he kept on the way he was going, Dean switched from bottles of Bud to IBC.

She still didn't speak, simply stared at the bottle in her hand. He scratched his head as she remained quiet. Didn't she want to talk? "Sarah, what is it?"

Sarah took another swallow, then cleared her throat. She looked up at him with those big eyes, took a deep breath and blurted, "Take me with you."

Dean wasn't sure what he expected, but it certainly wasn't that. "What?"

"You're leaving for Los Angeles in the morning, right?"

"Where did you hear that?"

"From Jennifer Krusick's son. I want to go with you."

"Sarah, I don't understand. If you want to go to California, you can drive there yourself. You don't want to ride on my bike."

"Yes, I do. Anyway, my car died this morning."

"Take a plane. It's a lot quicker too."

"I don't want quicker. I want interesting. I want exciting."

Heaven help him. Sarah Austin wanted excitement. "By the time we get to L.A. on my bike, your whole vacation will be gone."

"I have a lot of vacation time saved up."

"This is crazy."

She laughed, but it wasn't a light, happy sound. "I know. Please take me to L.A."

He frowned. There was desperation in her face, in her voice, and he didn't understand it. "Why do you want to go to California?"

She took a step closer to him. He could smell a light, flowery scent, probably from her hair. The shiny strands looked so soft he almost reached out to touch them before he caught himself and pulled his hand back. He stepped away before he could try it again.

"It doesn't matter why I want to go," she said, determination rising in her voice. "I'll pay for everything. All the gas. The food. The lodging. Everything."

"Sarah?" He stepped closer again, even though he knew he shouldn't. He must have been allergic to that scent she wore because he felt a little dizzy, a little off-center around her. "Are you in some kind of trouble?"

Some emotion he couldn't identify flashed in her eyes. "If you won't take me, I'll hitchhike."

"Be serious."

"I'm perfectly serious."

"Sarah, be sensible about this."

She started to shake and her face turned as red as it had this morning, but Dean could tell the difference between embarrassment and anger. This time he'd ticked her off royally.

But damn if she didn't look fine. This was not the meek and mild little Sarah he remembered sitting on her front porch with her nose in a book. This Sarah was vibrant and alive. Her eyes sparkled. Her skin glowed.

He wanted to know more about her. What had she been doing all these years? What was going on with her now?

He wanted to give in to the crazy urge to pull her into his arms and discover what her body felt like beneath the baggy clothes. He wanted to kiss her and find out what her passion tasted like.

As he entertained his lustful thoughts, he saw Sarah pull herself together. Drawing in a deep, shaky breath, she relaxed her clenched fists. She stared at him through narrowed eyes and set the root beer bottle on the coffee table.

"Thanks, anyway."

The regret on her face and in her voice seemed more a reflection on him, the one who'd protected her when she was young. Dean felt absurdly sorry to disappoint her.

She turned to leave, but she suddenly swayed and staggered. Dean reached out to catch her before her knees gave out. The distance between them was farther than he thought. He stretched out too far to catch her, lost his balance, and they both landed on the carpet.

She was soft and curvy beneath those clothes. That much registered as Dean held Sarah in his arms. He looked into her face. The blush was back. "Are you all right?"

She struggled to sit up. "I'm okay. Thanks...uh...for catching me."

"Have you had lunch yet?" he asked, not letting go of her. She felt way too good in his arms.

"No." She pushed him away from her and sat up.

"Well, what did you expect?" he asked. "Your body needs nourishment." He'd never admit to her that his lunch had consisted of his one addiction. Root beer.

She looked down at the hands clenched in her lap. "I guess you're right."

He reached over and took the bottle of root beer she'd set down. "Here, drink the rest of this. It's not nourishment, but it'll give your body some sugar for energy."

She took the bottle and raised it to her lips. Dean couldn't tear his eyes away from her slender throat as she swallowed again and again. When she lowered the bottle, her lips were wet and shiny and for a moment Dean almost leaned into them. What would Sarah taste like?

As if she heard his thoughts, she ran her tongue over those moist and tempting lips and he almost moaned out loud. Scrambling to his feet, he helped her up and tried not to look at her lips again. He had to clear his throat before he could speak. "I'd fix you something to eat, but there's nothing much here. Terry cleaned out the kitchen before she left."

"That's okay. I'll have a sandwich while I pack."

The little edge to her voice made him nervous all over again. "Pack for what?"

"I told you. I want to go to California. If you won't take me, I'm going to hitchhike. There must be someone going in that direction."

Her hands were shaking a little. Dean had to hope that meant she knew how foolhardy that idea was. He knew she said it in order to change his mind. He was afraid it was working.

"Sarah…"

"Don't you understand? If I don't do it now, I'll never do it."

He didn't understand, but he looked at her and remembered a little girl with long blonde braids and a tear-stained face, gazing up at him with hope in her eyes. And he could never forget how she beamed him with the smile that changed his life.

He'd do anything for her.

He sighed deep and loud, giving in to her emotional blackmail. "All right, Sarah. You win."

Her eyes sparkled. "Thank you."

He knew he was going to regret this. He traveled alone. Always had. Always would. Well, except this time. He didn't like the urge he had to take her in his arms. So, instead of returning her smile, he frowned.

"I don't suppose you have a helmet."

"No."

"Or leathers."

"What are leathers?"

"Or a rain suit."

She cocked her eyebrow as if to say, "Duh."

He sighed again, even deeper and louder. "I'd better get you a list of things you'll need."

She picked up the purse sitting on the floor and pulled out a pen and note pad. She stepped closer and handed them to him. "Okay, here."

He could smell her damn perfume again. He grabbed the paper and pen and started writing. Man, he was going to regret this.

🏍 🏍 🏍

"Don't worry, Mom, I'll be fine," Sarah said, looking up from her cup of tea. "I have to do this."

"No, you do not have to do this," Reva Austin said sharply, reaching out and gripping her daughter's hands. "What you have to do is take care of yourself."

Sarah sighed. "I will."

"I'm going to be so worried about you."

Sarah looked across the table at her mother. The worry lines her three children had etched in her face seemed deeper today. The weight of Reva's concern for her made her shoulders sag, but she wouldn't back down. Sarah gently pulled her hands away and wrapped them around her cup. "Don't be worried. I trust Dean. He travels all the time."

"Dean Bastian of all people. I remember when all you did was talk about him. Moon over him. Watch him out your bedroom window."

"Mom, that was years ago."

Her mother narrowed her eyes. "I don't care. You're asking for trouble. Why do you have to go with *him*?"

Running off with a sexy bad boy was a fantasy Sarah'd always had. Her mother would never understand her need for this trip. Her need for an adventure.

"I'm going with Dean because he's leaving in the morning and he said I could go with him." An excited thrill ran through her at the thought. "It's as simple as that."

"I doubt it's as simple as that." Her mother took a sip of her tea. "Honey, you're not up to this trip. Your health...I just don't think you can do it."

The old Sarah would have caved into her mother's wishes. After all, her mother did love her and wanted what was best for her, what was safe. But the new Sarah wanted more than safety. She'd lived her whole life playing it safe and what did she have to show for it? Nothing.

"I'm sorry you can't be excited for me, but I'm still going."

Tears shone in her mother's eyes. "How long will you be gone?"

"I don't know." The whole concept was unusual for her, yet kind of exciting at the same time. "I'll be going over the trip with Dean tonight. I don't even know how long it'll take us to get to California. And once I get out there, I guess I'll just have to see what happens."

"What do you mean by that?"

Sarah sighed. She was suddenly so tired. Her limbs felt as if they had weights attached to them. She had a long list of things to do before they left in the morning, but if she didn't get a chance to take a nap before she met Dean tonight, she'd never make it.

"I don't know, Mom. I don't know what I mean. I don't know what I want to do. My life's been turned upside down. I'm going to have to play it by ear for a while and see what happens."

"Play it by ear? My Sensible Sarah?" Her mother shook her head and laughed. "You'd never risk it. You were the one who had to know it all ahead of time."

"Well, I know better now. No one can know everything ahead of time, can they?"

Her mother was quiet for a moment, then she asked, "What did Dean say when you told him?"

"I didn't tell him."

Reva gasped. "Don't you think he should know?"

So he could feel sorry for her? The last thing Sarah wanted was Dean Bastian pitying her. "He doesn't need to know."

"Oh, Sarah."

"He doesn't need to know," she repeated.

"How can you be sure you can handle this?"

"Mom, have a little faith in me. There's no reason I shouldn't be able to ride on a motorcycle for a few days. And I'll still have time to do some sightseeing."

"How will you get home?"

That was an easy one. "I'll catch a flight when I'm ready to come back."

"You have a doctor's appointment on the sixteenth of next month.

"I know. I'll be back in plenty of time."

Reva rose and walked around the table. "I hope you know what you're doing."

Sarah stood up and hugged her mother. "Gotta go, Mom." She gave her a kiss on the cheek. "I have a lot to do. I have to shop and pack. I have a whole list of things to get at the Harley shop."

Thinking about all the things she still had to do made Sarah excited all over again. It was really happening. She was getting her adventure. She was really going to be riding a motorcycle across the United States.

And with Dean Bastian. Her teenage crush. The sexy rebel of her dreams. Who knew what kinds of situations they might end up in on the way.

Maybe she'd stop by Victoria's Secret, just in case.

Chapter Two

"Hey, Dean! That you?"

Dean looked up from the refrigerator case in the neighborhood convenience store. Sarah said she'd pick up the pizza for their little meeting tonight. He'd offered to get the root beer. Maybe he should pick up some aspirin too.

"Hey, Larry."

He hadn't seen Larry Brady since high school, not since senior homeroom and fifth period history class. Larry had always been tall and lean, but he'd packed on a few extra pounds in the last twelve years. A belly he didn't used to have hung over his belt. He held the hand of a little girl with dark curly hair, a shy smile and a pink dress. In his other hand he held a large package of diapers.

"Heard you were in town," Larry said. He set the diapers down on the floor and shook Dean's hand. "Staying long?"

He'd already been here longer than he wanted. "Leaving in the morning."

"Man, you have the life," Larry said, the envy clear in his voice. "Nothing ties you down, right?"

"Right." Dean fought to keep his expression blank. Larry would be disappointed if he knew the truth.

"Still drivin' the Harley?"

"Oh, yeah. I'd never give her up."

"So do you really live in California?" Larry made it sound like it was another country. "Heard you work for some rock band, slinging sound systems." A big grin split his face. "Heard chicks follow you around wherever you go."

The look on Larry's face said he wished it were true.

"Well," Dean said smoothly, "you can't believe everything you hear."

"Never got married?"

Now why did that suddenly sound sad? It was the way he wanted it. "No, never been married."

Larry sighed and then, as if he realized the impression he gave, swung the little girl up into his arms. She giggled, threw her arms around Larry's neck and planted a sloppy kiss on his cheek. A strange emotion swept over Dean, one he couldn't even name.

"This is Carly. We, that is, Lori and I, have a new baby boy too. Larry Junior. Only two months old."

What was it like to hold a new life in your arms? A life you helped create? If Sarah had a little girl, her eyes would be big and her hair blonde.

Whoa, where did that thought come from?

"She's beautiful," Dean said, tearing his thoughts away from Sarah and the children she didn't have. "And congratulations on the new baby."

"Man, if you were staying longer we could have gotten the guys together. You know, hit a few bars. You could tell us all the stories of your wild life."

"Yeah, man, too bad. Tell you what. Why don't you guys hit the bars anyway, and you can make up stories about me."

Larry laughed and set his little girl back down. "Yeah, right.

Well, gotta go. Lori's waiting for these." He hoisted the diapers. "Good to see you."

"Yeah, same here." Dean watched Larry and his little girl walk away hand in hand. He didn't know how long he stood there before the cold air from the beverage case started to give him a chill. He turned up the collar on his leather jacket and grabbed a six-pack of Mug's from the cooler.

His past would forever haunt him here. Everyone who knew him back then thought he was still the guy who sped through the neighborhood on his bike, daring the cops to catch him. The cocky rebel who thumbed his nose at authority, in school and out. The kid who hung out on the streets, nothing but a bad influence to all the other children.

It was too easy to fall back into the rebel persona he'd embraced from an early age. Dean had to admit, even now, there was something ego-boosting about seeing admiration and envy in the eyes of people like Larry Brady. If they got a charge out of believing he was still, at thirty, a hard-drinking, hard-living, rabble-rouser, who was he to disappoint them? If they got a charge out of thinking he traveled around the country with a rock band, partying with groupies every night, who was he to burst their bubble?

He could play the part with no trouble at all.

It was typical that everyone in the old neighborhood would remember the job he had for only one summer. No one seemed to know that he'd gone to college, much less that he graduated with honors. They probably wouldn't even believe him if he told them he had a full-time job as a counselor for troubled teens. That information wouldn't have fit in with who they thought he was.

But just because he had a respectable job didn't mean he wanted to settle down any further. The last thing he wanted was to be out buying diapers like good ol' Larry. Dean may not be a rebel or a roadie anymore, but settling down with one woman and raising a family? That's a future that would never work for him.

He got out of Buffalo a long time ago. He moved to Colorado after college to be near his sister and he loved it there. He felt he made a real difference in the lives of the kids he saw in the course of his work and he couldn't imagine doing anything else.

He could only run so far from his past, though. He may have escaped turning into his old man, but he'd never risk having a family. Not with the role model he had. Not with the memories of fists and fights and bottles of Bud.

He pushed away the memory of Larry with his little girl's arms around him. No, he was happy with things just the way they were.

When he reached the checkout, the cashier looked up at him through long lashes and blushed. All he did was smile at her. He'd made Sarah blush today too. He didn't understand it.

"Hi, there," he said, placing the six-pack on the counter. "Has anyone ever told you that you have beautiful hair?"

"Ah, n-n-no," she stammered, not meeting his eyes. She tucked a wayward strand of penny-red hair behind her ear before she rang up the soda and told him the price.

He passed over the bills and when she reached over to give him his change, he couldn't resist brushing his hand against her arm. She dropped the change.

"I'm sorry," she said, her face turning nearly as red as her hair.

"No, I'm sorry," Dean said. He bent down to pick up the coins that rolled near his boot. Damn. Why did he have to revert to being a jerk whenever he came back home?

He felt the eyes of everyone in the store on him when he walked out the door. He couldn't wait to leave this place. He'd only come back because Terry had pleaded. He'd finally agreed to come on the condition that he had the time to ride his bike out. If he had to go back for the funeral of a man he despised, at least he could enjoy the trip out.

But would he enjoy the trip back to Denver? What would it be like to travel all that way with Sarah riding behind him? He'd never ridden more than a short distance with someone behind him. He always traveled alone. He couldn't believe he told her she could come with him. What had he been thinking? Since when was it up to him to show Sarah Austin a little excitement?

He made it back to the house before Sarah got there. He'd given her quite a shopping list, but there were some essentials he wouldn't let her ride without. She'd looked surprised at the small saddlebag he gave her to pack everything in. He didn't have any choice. What with the camping gear and his stuff too, there wasn't much room left on the bike. He couldn't wait to see how she did with the shopping and packing.

In fact, he couldn't wait to see her, period.

That was a sudden, frightening thought. Sarah Austin hadn't entered his mind in years and now he couldn't get her out. He'd never thought about any of the women he'd dated over the years as much as Sarah'd been on his mind in the past few hours. Sarah with the big brown eyes and the desperation in her voice.

Frightening, very frightening.

He was out in the driveway, polishing the bike, when Sarah pulled up to the curb. At least, he thought it was Sarah. The woman who stepped out of the late-model Ford was petite, wearing faded blue jeans and a tight T-shirt that hugged her every curve. She pulled out a familiar saddlebag and slung it over her shoulder, then grabbed a pizza box out of the backseat. She nudged the door closed with her hip.

Dean couldn't take his eyes off her, or her new short, spiky hairdo. She looked sexy as hell. He felt his body tighten as her hips swayed in the well-washed denim. Her white T-shirt stretched seductively across her breasts and his heart pounded at the sight. They were only talking about the trip and he already couldn't control his response to her. They hadn't even left the driveway yet. What would happen once they were on the road? He felt more than a little irritated that he was so out of control around her.

"What did you do to your hair?" he called out, a little harsher than necessary.

Her bright smile faltered and she lost the little rhythm she'd had in her step. Real smooth, Bastian. She continued up the walk at a slower pace and Dean met her halfway. He took the pizza box out of her hands but she didn't meet his glance.

"I didn't mean that how it sounded," he told her. "You look great. In fact, I was blown away. You look so different."

She shrugged her shoulders and finally looked at him. "I can't fit a hairdryer in here," she said, pulling the saddlebag off her shoulder. "The stylist said I just use a little gel and I'm ready to go."

He'd always been one of those guys who loved women with long hair. Preferably flowing in a riot of curls down her back. But one look at Sarah and he was a changed man. The smooth pageboy she'd worn before had been plain and simple. But this flirty style brightened her eyes and flattered her tiny features. With a simple haircut, Sarah had been transformed from merely pretty to palm-tingling sexy.

He wanted to touch her again. Really touch her this time. Play with the fringe of hair around her face. Nibble on her pretty little ears. Kiss the bare nape of her neck. He grasped both ends of the pizza box. He was in big trouble.

He tore his eyes away from her and tried to focus on something else, anything else. The car. That was a safe subject. He nodded toward the sedan she'd driven up in. "I thought your car died."

Sarah followed his gaze to the curb. "It's Mom's. She let me borrow it tonight."

"Oh. Yeah, I noticed she doesn't live on the street anymore."

"After Dad died, she sold the house and moved into an apartment. Less upkeep for her."

Dean nodded and carried the pizza down the broken concrete walk to the house. Sarah didn't follow him up to the porch. Instead, she crossed the grass and stood beside his bike.

"So this is it," she said. She ran one hand over the seat, the saddlebag hanging from her other hand. "It's beautiful." Dean watched her from the porch, the pizza box warm in his hands. She was beautiful. She turned to look at him, her smile lighting up her face again. "Wow, I can't believe I'm doing this."

Dean couldn't believe it either. "Let's eat before it gets cold. We'll get her packed up after dinner."

She followed him into the house. He set the pizza box on the kitchen counter and pulled a couple plates from the cupboard. "Help yourself."

She stopped at the table and stared at the map of the United States that was spread on the table. With one slender finger, she traced a crow's-fly route from Buffalo to Los Angeles. "Wow, it's a long way, isn't it?"

"Over twenty-five-hundred miles."

She nodded and stared at the map. Dean served her up a

piece of pizza and set the plate in front of her. His mouth watered, and if she noticed, he'd swear it was from the great-smelling pizza.

"L.A.?" Dean asked. He backed away before he did something stupid like kiss her neck. "Is that where you want to go?"

She nodded again, then turned to look at him with a frown. "Isn't that where you're headed?"

He looked up from the fridge. "Well, actually, I need to go to Denver."

"Denver, but...oh, of course, that's where the next gig is, right? That's the right word, isn't it? Gig?"

The words were on the tip of his tongue. The words to tell her the truth. But he knew she'd be disappointed if she heard them. She wanted to believe he was still the bad boy, just like everyone else. And Dean found himself wanting to do anything to stop her from being disappointed. He'd do anything to keep that smile on her face. So he left the words unsaid. "Right."

"Well, I can't ask you to go all the way to Los Angeles if you're not going there. I'll ride to Denver with you."

He came up and stood behind her. He told himself it was to look over her shoulder at the map. He didn't want to admit, even to himself, that he wanted to be close enough to catch her scent again. "But how will you get where you need to go?"

"I'll figure something out." Sarah took a step back and bumped into him.

His hands came up by instinct and grabbed her shoulders. Maybe it was his imagination, but he thought she leaned into him for a moment before she jerked away and he dropped his hands back down to his side.

"Sorry," she said, her voice a little breathless. "I didn't

realize you were so close."

"Just trying to see the map." He leaned over to straighten out the map and brushed against her arm. "Maybe we should sit down and I'll go over the route with you."

"Okay." Was it his imagination this time when she brushed against his arm before she sat down in the chair? Or did he brush against her?

"Denver is almost across the country, isn't it?" she asked as they sat down. "That will be okay. Show me how we'll get there."

They sat beside each other at the table, shoulder to shoulder. Dean felt the heat from her body and they weren't even touching. Or maybe it was the heat he knew he would feel if he ever got the chance to touch Sarah the way he ached to.

The way he knew he shouldn't. The way he couldn't.

"It's pretty simple, really," Dean said, trying to get his mind back on the trip and off sweet-smelling Sarah. "We'll hit the thruway, take 90 down to 79, then take that to 70. See? It's a straight shot. We take 70 all the way to Denver."

"Wait a minute," Sarah said, turning to look at him. She was so close, he could see the individual lashes framing her lovely eyes. She'd picked up her slice of pizza, but now she slowly placed it back on her plate. "Are you saying we're going to be taking the interstate the whole way?"

"It's the only way to make time."

"I don't want to make time," Sarah said, with that hint of desperation in her voice again. "I want to make memories."

Dean frowned. What was going on? There had to be more to Sarah's story than what she'd told him so far. "Memories? What are you talking about?"

"How can I see new towns and new people if we stay on the

interstate?"

Dean felt a headache coming on. He should have picked up that aspirin. "Hold on a sec. You said you wanted a ride. You didn't say you wanted to see all the towns along the way."

"Well, I do," Sarah said. She pushed her chair away from the table and bounded to her feet. "What's wrong with that? What's the point of traveling if you can't experience new things along the way?"

She was right, of course. Dean thought exactly the same thing. Life was a journey and you had to enjoy the trip. But how much time could he realistically give her? He had a job to go back to. Even though his boss had told him to take as much time as he needed, he didn't want to push his luck.

The real question was how long could he travel with Sarah and not touch her as he'd been longing to do since he'd set eyes on her this morning?

Was it only this morning?

What kind of man would he be if he took advantage of Sarah while they traveled together? She trusted him to take her where she wanted to go. He wasn't going to take that trust lightly. She wasn't a quick fling kind of girl. If there was ever a woman who was made for white picket fences and bunches of kids, it was Sarah. He may be his father's son, but he damn well wasn't his father.

He stood up and turned to face her. There could be no kissing, even though he thirsted to taste her lips. No fondling, even though his fingers itched with the need to touch her soft skin. No warming up the sleeping bag together on this trip. But the thought of making love with Sarah, of feeling her wriggle beneath him, hearing her soft whimpers of delight, made his body harden. She was still looking at him, waiting for a reply.

"I only have so much time. I can't stay away from work

indefinitely."

He was fascinated by the play of emotions that danced across her face as annoyance gave way to embarrassment. "Oh, you're right. I'm sorry. I wasn't thinking. Of course, you have to get back to your job." But she couldn't mask the disappointment that clouded her eyes.

How could he turn her down, even if it meant he'd be tempted by her for a day or two longer? "Tell you what. If we can get a good start tomorrow, I don't have any problem with getting off the interstate now and then along the way."

There was that smile again. Without any conscious thought, Dean lifted his hand and lightly touched her cheek. Soft. Perfect. He knew he didn't imagine it this time when she leaned into his caress.

Then she stepped away. And looked away.

Damn. It only took him about two seconds to start acting like a jerk again. He shoved his hands in the pockets of his jeans.

"Do we need to make hotel reservations for tomorrow night?" She looked out the window to where his bike sat in the driveway.

"No, we'll be camping. We shouldn't have any trouble finding a campsite when we're ready to turn in."

"Camping?" She said it slowly, as if she were testing the sound of it. "I've never been camping."

"You'll love it." Well, he loved it. He hoped she would too. "Lots of fresh air. Sitting around the campfire." He pulled out her chair for her and she sat back down. "You want to meet people? Stop at a campground with a motorcycle. People will be coming to meet us."

Her eyes lit up again. "Really?"

"Sure."

She slowly reached out and touched his cheek, a fleeting touch before her hand was back down at her side. "Thanks for taking me, Dean."

After they'd finished the pizza, Sarah followed Dean outside to get the bike ready for the morning. Because they'd be leaving at first light, they needed to have everything packed tonight. She stood next to the bike, taking in all the chrome, paint and leather. It was beautiful, the chrome shining with the setting sun. It was bigger than she thought it would be, too, wide and heavy.

Yet it also looked terribly vulnerable. There was nothing to shield the rider from the windstorm of a passing tractor-trailer. There were no reinforced doors for protection during a crash. No air bags. No seat belts. None of the safety features everyone said was necessary to safely travel on the highways and country roads of this world.

And she was going to cross the United States on this thing? What was she thinking? How could anyone survive that many miles on a motorcycle?

She tried to calm the panic suddenly rising up in her throat. This was ridiculous. She wasn't going to chicken out at the first hint of danger. People traveled by motorcycle every day. Dean had survived all of his motorcycle trips and he didn't look any the worse for wear. In fact, he looked great.

She watched him attach the saddlebags to the bike. When he bent over, Sarah had a perfect view of his really nice butt. It was enough to get her mind off all sorts of safety issues. Wow. She watched the denim stretch across his thighs and her body tingled. In fact, she'd been super-aware of him ever since she pulled up to his curb this evening.

Were these leftover vibes from her teenage crush? Dean was the first guy she'd been attracted to, but he wasn't the only one. She'd dated other men. Touched and kissed other men, which was more than she'd done with Dean. She'd even had sex with a couple guys, but she never reacted to any of them the way she did to Dean.

Looking back at the guys she'd been with, she had to be honest with herself. They were boring men. Safe men. She'd never really risked her heart.

But Dean was different from all those other guys. He was the rebel, the bad boy. He wasn't looking for steady relationships like those other guys were. And like she had been looking for at the time.

But things had changed. Her whole life had changed. Tears sprang to her eyes as she realized that she would never have that kind of relationship now. She would never marry or have children. She vowed she would never burden anyone with the future that lay before her.

Dean stood up and turned around. Sarah blinked and looked away before he could notice the tears.

"What's wrong?"

Too late. She wiped at her eyes and smiled sheepishly. "Nothing's wrong."

He was at her side in a heartbeat. The concern on his face was touching and seemed out of character for a rebellious bad boy. "Sarah, what is it?"

"Nothing. Really. I feel so foolish." She turned her back to him until she was sure the tears were gone. "I'm tired. And a little nervous, I guess. I'll be fine."

He raised an eyebrow, but he didn't push it. "How about a trial ride? Let's take a quick spin before we call it a night."

Nerves swooped in her stomach. "A spin?"

"Just down to the gas station. I want to fill up."

Her immediate reaction was to say, "No, thanks." She'd wait until she *had* to get on that thing. But that was the old Sarah talking. The new Sarah jumped at opportunities to try new things. She embraced new experiences. Even ones with no safety features.

Like a relationship with Dean?

No, not a relationship. Sex. A hot, no-strings fling on the road.

That thought was enough to stop Sarah in her tracks. He was watching her, his blue eyes piercing, as if he was trying to read her thoughts. What would he say if he knew she was considering a sex fest on the road? If she read his body language right, maybe he wouldn't even be surprised. He'd be thrilled, wouldn't he? He was a guy after all. A love 'em and leave 'em kind of guy. It was perfect.

"Are you sure you're okay?"

He was so sexy with that concerned look on his face. She had to stop making him nervous. Or did she?

She walked slowly over to him, swaying her hips, and stopped a little closer to him than she was comfortable with. "Promise me it will be safe?"

"I'm a safe driver, Sarah. Don't worry." He smiled and she felt weak in the knees. A weakness she knew had nothing to do with her condition. "Come on," he said, his voice suddenly low and seductive. "You haven't lived 'til you've slid a Harley between your thighs."

She stared at him for a moment as the tingles from all over her body congregated deep within her. There was a challenge in his eyes and she was definitely up for it. "I'll get my helmet."

"Grab your jacket too," he said. "The sun will be down soon."

"Okay." She snatched them out of the car, suddenly trembling with excitement.

"Long pants and a jacket aren't only protection from the cool night air," Dean said. She watched him put his helmet on, then did the same, fumbling a little with the strap. "If we were to lay the bike down, it's protection against the pavement."

Lay the bike down? "You mean wipe out?" There was enough of the old Sarah left to make her take a step backward. "We're not going to wipe out, are we?"

She fell hard for his devilish grin. "Of course not."

Dean smoothly straddled the bike with his long legs. Then he smiled and patted the seat behind him. It was a little awkward climbing on with her shorter legs, but she steadied herself by grabbing on to his shoulders, and before she knew it, she was actually sitting on a Harley.

She faced the broad expanse of his back. Dean pointed out the strap on the seat she could hold on to, but she couldn't resist the urge to put her arms around him when he started the engine. She felt his firm abs quiver when her hands rested there. The loud rumble of the engine pulsed through her. The vibration of the motorcycle itself ran through her, gathering deep in her core. Hey, this was as good as that vibrator in the drawer of her nightstand.

She tightened her grip on Dean as they took off down the driveway and out onto the street. As they leaned into the turn, it was almost like a carnival ride and she was afraid for a moment that she was going to lose her balance. She felt a little vulnerable with the wind blowing by her on both sides. What if they did lay the bike down?

Gradually, as she gained her balance, the nervousness

disappeared. Feeling alive for the first time in ages, she let out a whoop.

Dean glanced back at her and grinned.

She whooped again, from the sheer thrill of the ride and from Dean's infectious grin. She leaned into his back and hugged him tight. She could get used to holding him. Was she crazy to consider a fling with Dean?

No more crazy than what she was doing right now. In fact, she'd be crazy not to take advantage of these next few days with Dean.

They went down the road a few blocks to the gas station and Sarah watched Dean fill up the tank, careful not to let any gas drip on his bike. He even used a rag to wipe off the finish when he was done. She teased him about it, but he just smiled and started up the engine.

They were back to his house way too soon.

"Ready for the morning?" Dean asked after he removed his helmet.

Sarah tossed her helmet up in the air and caught it. "Oh, yeah. I can see why you love it." The next few days lay before her, exciting and filled with possibilities. And the night, and all its possibilities, stretched before them now. "I can't wait to start."

"Well, we'd better get a good night's sleep. It'll be sunrise before you know it." He gave her a wave, dismissing her. "See you in the morning. Bright and early."

"I've been thinking," Sarah said before she could chicken out, "since we're leaving so early in the morning..." She forced herself to look Dean in the eye and give him her most endearing smile. "Maybe I should spend the night here."

Chapter Three

What was she trying to do? Kill him? Sure, she could spend the night here with him. They could get reacquainted in his bed. He already knew how soft she would feel in his arms. He could imagine the taste of her sweet lips and feel the weight of her breasts in his hands. He could picture them tangled in his sheets, breathing heavily, bringing each other to a frenzied climax over and over again, all through the night. Hell, they might be too tired to take the bike out until much later in the day.

It would be worth it to have soft, sweet Sarah beneath him.

He pushed that picture far, far away. "You have to take the car back to your mom," he reminded her, his voice passion-rough although he'd done nothing but stand on the blacktop driveway mere inches away from her. "I'll pick you up in the morning."

He stopped breathing when she reached out and smoothed back a strand of hair that had fallen into his face. Her touch was soft, yet sent shivers along his skin.

"She has to drop me off somewhere," Sarah said. "My apartment or your house. What's the difference?"

Temptation across town or temptation in his house. Big difference. "Sarah..."

The sun had nearly disappeared below the horizon, but the glow from the streetlight threw an alluring beam across her face.

"This way you won't have to go out of your way to pick me up in the morning," she said. The beam of light picked up her slow smile. "I'll be right here."

Right here. Dean was so hard already he doubted he could walk into the house without a limp. How could he sleep a wink knowing she was in the same house with him? He wouldn't be worth a damn in the morning. "Sarah..."

"It's just for sleeping, right?" Her voice was soft and seductive, slowly talking him into this bad idea. "Everything's already packed. It'll be more convenient for us in the morning if I'm already here."

He balled his hands into fists to stop himself from reaching out and pulling her into his arms right then and there. He refused to revert back to the jerk.

She took another step closer, although there was barely any space between them as it was. "You know I'm right," she whispered. "Don't fight it, Dean."

He couldn't reply. He could barely breathe. He certainly couldn't fight.

She winked, turned on her heels and sauntered away from him. "I'll be back soon," she called over her shoulder.

He hadn't moved by the time she pulled the car away from the curb and drove off.

Don't fight it, Dean. What did she mean by that? What shouldn't he fight? Sarah spending the night here? Or their growing attraction for each other?

Sarah's heart pounded as she drove away. She'd never

been so bold in her entire life. If she hadn't been certain of Dean's attraction to her, she never would have acted like she did. Never would have practically come right out and offered herself to him. But this was her time and she was going to make it count. And, with Dean, she wouldn't have to worry about all the other concerns of a new relationship, especially an intimate one.

Did he love her? Would he be faithful? Would he want to get married some day? Would he leave and break her heart?

She didn't have to worry about any of those things. She already knew they had no future together. They only had the next few days.

What a trip this was going to be. She was as excited about having a fling with Dean as she was to climb on that motorcycle and see the country. She'd make enough memories to last her the rest of her life.

Clouds gathered in the darkening sky. She could feel the threat of rain in the air when she got out of the car at her mother's apartment building.

Her mom was waiting at the door of her first-floor apartment. "Is everything ready to go?" she asked.

Sarah nodded. She took a deep breath before she said to her mother, "I need you to drop me off at Dean's."

Reva simply looked at her for a moment, then nodded. Sarah could see the worry in her eyes. "I guess you're old enough to know what you're doing."

She couldn't help but grin when she handed her mother the car keys.

Reva picked up her purse and opened the door. She turned to look at Sarah. "How will you carry your purse?"

"No purse." Sarah pointed to the nylon pack strapped

around her waist. "My wallet and cell phone are in here."

A little thrill of anticipation swept through her when her mother started the car. This was it. She was starting her adventure.

"I can't help but worry, you know," her mother said. She didn't take her hands off the steering wheel or her eyes off the road. "Your situation is a little different from other daughters who decide to run off with a guy they barely know."

Sarah ignored the part about her situation and said, "I've known Dean my whole life. Don't worry. It's only for a few days."

Reva nodded and in a few minutes they pulled up in front of his house. Another thrill ran through Sarah that had everything to do with seeing Dean again.

"I love you, Mom." Sarah leaned over and kissed her mother's cheek. She took a deep, shaky breath and patted her waist pack. "I'll call you along the way."

"I do hope you have a wonderful time, sweetheart. But be smart, please."

Right now nervous knots twisted in her stomach and she wondered how smart she really was. "I will."

Dean left the porch light on for her. The wind had picked up and whipped around her. Leaves swirled around her ankles. For the first time she could remember, the wind didn't blow pieces of hair into her eyes and mouth. She climbed the steps and Dean opened the door before she had a chance to knock.

"Hi," he said.

He looked like he'd just gotten out of the shower. His wet hair was pulled back into a ponytail at the nape of his neck. His jeans rode low on his hips. His feet were bare. And so was his chest. He held his shirt in his hand.

"Come on in."

She realized she hadn't moved from her spot on the porch. She had to get a grip. They were pretty much going to be living together for the next few days. Sleeping together. She couldn't freeze simply at the sight of his incredibly gorgeous pecs.

She walked into the living room and Dean closed the door behind her. The house was quiet, the room shadowed. Thunder rumbled in the distance. Her heart galloped in her chest. She stood in the middle of the floor, not certain what to do next. Dean was right. She probably should have stayed at her place tonight.

Sarah watched Dean pull on his shirt, fascinated by the muscles that flexed and bunched at the simple task. Then he turned and walked into the kitchen. "Thirsty?" he asked. "There's some root beer left."

"Thanks."

She followed him into the kitchen for want of something else to do. She had the crazy urge to pull that shirt back off his body and cover his chest with her hands instead. What would that warm skin feel like beneath her palms? What would it taste like on her tongue? She hung back, afraid for a moment that she'd actually do it. Even the new Sarah wasn't quite that bold yet.

He'd folded up all the maps and they sat in a pile on the end of the table. The tall stack was a symbol of the distance they'd be traveling. The distance she'd go. "How far do you think we'll get tomorrow?"

"I'd like to stay on the interstate tomorrow." He handed her a bottle, but didn't meet her eye. "With any luck at all we should get through Pennsylvania and Ohio."

"Okay."

She followed him back into the living room and sat down beside him on the well-worn sofa. He glanced over at her, but didn't say anything for a moment. Then he cleared his throat.

"Uh, Sarah, about what you said about paying for all the food and gas and stuff. You don't have to do that."

"Yes, I do. I mean, I want to. You wouldn't be going to all this trouble if it wasn't for me."

"You're no trouble." But his expression said otherwise. She was imposing on him, and she knew it. The dark shadows in his eyes hinted that he was attracted to her and he didn't like it. But he obviously wasn't about to talk about that, either. "We can each pay for our own food and we can take turns on the gas and camping fees."

"Dean, let me do this," she said, putting her hand on his arm. She tried not to think about how good it felt there. "You're driving the whole way. I can't give you a break driving the motorcycle."

"You don't drive a motorcycle."

She was surprised by the little sarcastic bite in his voice. "What?"

"You don't drive a bike. You ride it."

Same difference as far as she was concerned. "Oh, well, anyway, the least I can do is pay."

"But, Sarah..."

"Listen, Dean. I've worked full-time since I got out of high school. I have a tiny apartment and I've had the same car since twelfth grade." She paused, remembering the tow truck hauling it away this morning. Was it only this morning? "Well, I *had* that car. What I'm getting at is that I haven't spent all that much. All I've done is save my money for a rainy day." She looked out the window and saw the wet drops hitting the pane. "And, damn, if it isn't raining."

Dean looked as if he was about to say something else, but

he shook his head and looked away. The subject might come up again later, but she felt as if she'd won the first round.

She eased her hand off his arm and wrapped it around the soda bottle. "Do you think it'll still be raining in the morning?"

He shrugged his shoulders, still looking straight ahead at nothing. "The storms are supposed to be through by morning."

"I hope so."

He turned to look at her with a frown. "You packed your rain suit, didn't you?"

"Yes, but the thought of losing control of the bike on wet pavement makes me a little nervous."

He frowned even deeper and shadows clouded his eyes again. If she didn't know him, she'd almost be afraid. "I'm not going to lose control," he growled.

How well *did* she really know him? Was she foolish *not* to be afraid?

His face went blank. "You know, if this trip makes you nervous, you can still book a plane."

She took his hand. "No. The trip doesn't make me nervous. It makes me excited."

He shook his head and looked away again. She dropped his hand.

"I don't want to fly across the country," she went on. "I want to see the country."

"I know." He was probably thinking about how much trouble she was going to be on this trip. Sarah vowed right then and there to be absolutely no trouble to Dean in the next few days.

She took the chance in the silence that followed to study him close up. His was a strong profile. The good-looking boy she remembered had turned into a handsome man. His face wasn't smooth—it sported a few laugh lines and frown lines, probably from riding in the sun a lot. But it was all the more attractive because it was the face of a man who lived. A man who laughed and frowned, who flew down the highway in the sunshine and made her body long for his touch.

The sound of his deep breathing washed over her. What did it mean that her own breathing fell into rhythm with his? Was his heart pounding as hard as hers? Was his body also on fire with need?

When she couldn't ignore the desire burning within her any longer, she placed her bottle on the coffee table and slowly turned to face him.

"Damn." The word came out of Dean's mouth on a sigh.

He set his bottle down as well and turned to her. In one smooth movement, he cupped her face with his hands. His lips were on hers almost before she had a chance to breathe.

His hands were cool and damp on her face, but his lips were hot and wet. Hot and wet and needy. They slid across her mouth, teasing her with his taste. His tongue followed the path, coaxing her lips apart. When he deepened the kiss, plunging into her mouth, she drank him in, her whimpers mixing with his moan.

Sarah combed her fingers through his hair, enjoying the way the silky strands slid along her skin. When it loosened from the ponytail, she spread it across his shoulders. She held his head in her hands, meeting each thrust of his tongue with an eager one of her own. She leaned closer, needing to touch him more, longing to feel his hands on her.

Waves of awareness ran along her skin, gathering into a pool of need within her. She was drowning in his kisses, but she needed more. She lowered her hands, skimming his neck, kneading his shoulders.

A crack of lightning lit up the sky and the deafening roll of thunder followed almost immediately. Dean broke away and leapt to his feet. He gasped for air. Odd, she still matched him breath for breath.

"I put clean sheets on Terry's old bed," he said, his voice ragged. "You can sleep there tonight."

Of course, he wouldn't want to talk about the kiss. Or the need. "Dean?"

He backed away from her. His eyes were still shadowed, his expression grim. "Go to bed, Sarah, before you cause any more trouble."

She knew the new Sarah would stay and argue, would stick to her guns and say that he started the kiss to begin with and he caused his own damn trouble. But there was too much of the old Sarah in her and the thought of Dean pushing her away again hurt so badly that she simply turned and walked up the stairs without saying a word.

Dean gave up trying to sleep about the same time the thunderstorm gave up its hold on western New York. Knowing Sarah was in the next room, most likely tossing and turning on his sister's old mattress, was enough to make him forget any chance of relaxing tonight.

He got up and left the bedroom and the reminder that there was a chance he could have had Sarah in here on his mattress tonight. He paced from the living room to the kitchen and back again, chastising himself for his behavior with Sarah.

He'd kissed her. How could he be so stupid? After all his vows to keep his hands off her, he'd caressed her face, captured her lips. After his promise to himself not to be a jerk, he'd gone ahead and done it anyway.

But she'd tasted so sweet. She'd felt so soft, so right. He couldn't get her taste off of his lips. His hands still tingled from wanting to touch her again.

He stopped pacing and looked out the living room window. It was still too dark to see his bike or anything else out there. But as soon as it was light, they would be mounting that motorcycle together and spending days together. And nights together. Would he be able to keep his hands, and other body parts, to himself?

Of course, she wanted it too, the old bad boy hurried to remind him. She dove into that kiss with a passion to equal his own. Her hands had been all over him. She wasn't the one who broke away, he was.

Yeah, he could have had her in his bed tonight. They could have worked out their frustration the old-fashioned way and gotten a good night's sleep in each other's arms.

It didn't matter. It was up to him to make sure the situation didn't get out of hand again. Sarah was in some kind of trouble. Maybe she didn't trust him enough to confide in him yet, but he knew this trip was something more to her than a taste of excitement.

And how could she ever trust him, if he couldn't even trust himself around her?

"Dean?"

He turned from the window and saw Sarah standing at the foot of the stairs. The oversized T-shirt she wore dipped off one shoulder and barely skimmed the top of her thighs. Her hair stuck out at odd angles, but for some reason it simply made her look even more appealing.

"Are you okay?" she asked.

His mouth was so dry he could barely swallow. In fact, he could only nod at first, because no words could force themselves past the enormous lump in his throat.

"I couldn't sleep either."

He noticed that her eyes roamed over his body and she began to chew on that lower lip of hers. That's when Dean remembered he was only wearing boxer shorts. Damn, could he do anything else to sabotage all his good intentions?

He cleared his throat. "I'm sorry about last night," he said, his voice still a little rough.

She narrowed her eyes. "You're not apologizing for kissing me, are you?" He opened his mouth to reply but she plowed right ahead. "Am I a bad kisser?"

He nearly laughed. He still couldn't think straight because of that kiss. "Of course not."

"Then why are you sorry you kissed me?"

"That has nothing to do with it. I had no business kissing you."

She propped her hands onto her hips, hiking the purple tie-dyed T-shirt even higher. "Why not?"

"Sarah..."

"If you tell me to be sensible, I'm going strangle you."

"Look at it this way," Dean said, crossing the room and coming closer to her than he probably should. "We are going to be traveling together for several days."

"And nights," she added.

Those nights were already haunting him. "Exactly. We don't need to complicate things by adding a physical relationship to the mix."

"I see." The confused expression on her face said otherwise. "A kiss complicates things?"

"Yes, it does."

"How does a kiss complicate our trip?"

Dean sighed. His brain was fuzzy from lack of sleep and too much untapped sexual energy. He wasn't up to playing word games with Sarah at two in the morning. "I can't even sleep tonight because of that kiss. That's going to affect my driving tomorrow."

She nodded, but he couldn't quite decipher the look on her face. "I see what you mean. I'm sorry, Dean. Next time you try to kiss me, I'll slap your face."

"Very funny," he said, frowning. "There won't be a next time. You can be sure of that." He reached out and pulled the T-shirt up onto her bare shoulder. It was either that or pull the whole thing off. "Now go get some sleep. I don't want you falling off the back of the bike tomorrow."

Sarah finally fell asleep sometime before dawn. When Dean's knock on the bedroom door woke her up, she knew she hadn't slept nearly long enough. Dean didn't get much sleep either, she reminded herself as she gathered her things together. She couldn't help but smile, knowing she'd done that to him.

She washed up quickly, only fumbling slightly with the toothbrush. She threw on jeans and a bright red T-shirt. The gel worked wonders with her hair. Sarah wished she'd done this years ago. The woman in the mirror with the spiky hair didn't look anything like a sensible person who worked at a bank. This woman fit right in with the image of leather jackets and motorcycles.

It still blew her mind that this woman was her. That she was jumping on a motorcycle and riding to Denver, Colorado. Who could have guessed yesterday morning, when her car broke down and her depression was getting to her, that today she would be starting her adventure?

Could Dean be right? Would their attraction for each other cause them trouble on this trip? She honestly never thought he would actually resist the attraction they felt for each other. She figured he would have jumped at the chance for a roll in the hay with a willing woman.

Sarah made the bed, marveling at the direction her thoughts were taking her. She and Dean hadn't seen each other in years, had only met up again less than twenty-four hours ago. Since when was she actually contemplating having sex with someone she'd been with for less than twenty-four hours?

She knew exactly since when. But boy, this new Sarah was a whole different person from the Sensible Sarah she'd been for way too long. She was never quite sure how she was going to react to anything.

Dean was waiting for her when she came down the stairs. He looked overwhelmingly sexy in his black jeans and white T-shirt. He held the pile of maps and his black leather jacket in his hand. "Ready?"

"Aren't we going to have any breakfast?" she asked.

"I'd like to get on the road for a couple hours. By then we'll be ready for a stop and we can get something to eat. Sound okay to you?"

"Sure."

Just like that they left Buffalo, New York behind. Sarah didn't look back. She looked forward. She was not only going forward into her adventure, she was going forward into her new life, the one that scared the hell out of her.

She laughed out loud when they left the city streets behind and got on the thruway. She held onto Dean as they flew down the road. The fresh air and speed blew the fear out of her mind.

Take that! she cried silently to the monster that had already taken over her body. She wasn't going to let it frighten her today. She wasn't going to dwell on her future for as long as this trip took.

She'd have the whole rest of her life to deal with the fact that she had multiple sclerosis.

Chapter Four

The world looked different to Sarah from the back of a Harley. Everything was more up close and personal. More real than riding in air-conditioned comfort, looking at the world through tinted windows.

As the miles flew past, Sarah settled into her seat. She now felt comfortable enough to stop gripping Dean every second, but she liked the feel of holding onto him anyway.

They left New York before they stopped for breakfast. Not long into Pennsylvania, they pulled off one of the Erie exits to eat. As much as she had been enjoying the ride, Sarah was relieved when Dean pulled into the restaurant parking lot. Her butt was numb and her stomach was growling.

She could tell something was wrong as soon as she tried to get off the motorcycle. Her leg felt like dead weight. When she tried to swing it over the seat, her foot landed with a thud on the pavement and buckled beneath her. She crumpled to the ground before she could catch herself.

Dean reached her in an instant, kneeling beside her. "Are you all right?"

She tried to laugh it off even though she wanted to sit there and cry. Did she actually think she could escape her diagnosis? It sure hadn't taken long for her to realize that running hadn't gotten her any farther away from her problems. She should have known they'd follow her no matter where she went. They weren't going to be left behind.

Dean put his arm around her and helped her to her feet. She prayed her legs would hold her. "My butt's numb," she said, holding his arm for support. "My legs are too, I guess."

"It takes a little while to get used to riding long distances," he told her. They walked slowly toward the restaurant, his arm around her waist. "We'll stop every couple hours and walk a little. You'll have an iron butt before you know it."

Sarah had to laugh. "Iron butt, yeah, that sounds real attractive."

Dean stopped suddenly and leaned back, obviously looking at the current subject of discussion. "I'd say it's real attractive already."

She punched him in the shoulder. She felt her face heat up, but if he noticed her blush, he didn't say anything about it.

"There is an Iron Butt Award, you know," he went on. "You get it for riding a thousand miles in twenty-four hours."

Sarah stopped and stared at him. "How is that possible?"

He shrugged. "No sleep."

"I think I like my sleep too much."

His eyes twinkled. "Yeah, me too."

Eggs, ham and juice went a long way toward improving Sarah's mood. And she had to admit to herself that Dean's compliment boosted her spirits as much as the food. She and Dean actually chatted companionably over breakfast, with Dean telling her some stories of other trips he'd taken on his bike.

She noticed he never mentioned anyone else in his tales of the road. "Do you ever take trips with someone else?"

He shook his head. "I'm pretty much a loner. I like going my own way." He took a sip of coffee. "I guess you could call me selfish. I don't want to have to bow to someone else's wishes. My time is precious to me and I don't want to waste it doing something I don't want to do."

A chill washed over Sarah. So she was an inconvenience already. She stared at him.

"What?" he asked, frowning.

"Like you're wasting your time now?"

He cursed under his breath. "That's not what I meant."

"That's what you said."

She pushed her chair away from the table and stood up, gripping the table to make sure her legs were going to cooperate before she let go. She'd already vowed she wasn't going to be a burden to anyone.

"Take my things off the bike," she said through gritted teeth. "I'm sure I can find someone going west to hitch a ride with."

Dean stood up too. "Sarah, I didn't mean you. I didn't mean this trip."

Sarah pulled some bills out of her wallet and threw enough to cover the food and tip on the table. She grabbed her helmet and started toward the door. Dean stepped in front of her. She held out the helmet, but he didn't take it. He grasped her shoulders and looked into her eyes.

"This trip is *not* something I don't want to do," he said, speaking slowly and deliberately. "Believe it or not, I'm actually looking forward to it. Looking forward to traveling with you." He smiled wryly. "Don't ask my why, but I *want* to do this."

Sarah didn't say anything for a moment, but just studied him. His hands were still on her shoulders. His expression looked sincere, even if he also seemed to be a little uncomfortable. He probably didn't make too many admissions like that.

"Time is too precious," she said softly, echoing his words. "I don't want to be wasting yours."

He didn't break eye contact with her. "I told you, you won't be."

She wanted to believe him and so she nodded. "Okay."

A group of people came in the front doors and looked curiously at them as they walked by. Dean dropped his hands and stepped back. "Listen, we'll drive 'til the middle of the afternoon, then find a campground. We don't want to overdo on your first day."

Sarah nodded. Even though she'd love to say they could go as long as he wanted, she knew she'd reach her limit sooner than he would. "Sounds like a plan."

"We'll go over the map tonight and you can pick the route for tomorrow."

"And I won't be wasting your time if I want to drive through all the little towns and stop to eat at local diners and shop at little boutiques along the way?"

Dean lifted an eyebrow. "Don't forget that whatever you buy has to fit in your saddlebag."

"You're no fun." But she smiled when she said it. Actually, she had the feeling Dean might turn out to be a whole lot of fun.

Dean fed another log on the campfire. It wouldn't be dark for a little while yet, but he always liked to sit by a campfire. The primal pull of the flames or something. He turned from where he sat on the picnic table bench and looked over at

Sarah. She sat on a folded-up sleeping bag, bent over some little book, scribbling like mad. Her journal, she said.

He'd never seen the need to keep track of something you'd already done. Once you'd lived it, what was the point of going back? Why read about it later?

He couldn't stop watching her, though. Streaks of her golden hair glinted in the sun. And, bent over like she was, the sun also threw an interesting shadow across her chest, hinting at what was beneath that colorful shirt.

He could still feel her hands on him today. His muscles twitched at the thought. For hours on end he rode, trying to ignore her soft touch, her warm breath on his neck. He hadn't done anything stupid, but it would have been too easy to be distracted by her. By simply knowing she was right behind him, close enough to kiss if he'd been able to turn around and find her lips.

Her lips. Wet and shiny lips. She chewed on that bottom lip again, intent on the words she wrote. She glanced up from her journal and caught him looking at her. Had she felt him watching her? Did she know how much he wanted to sit down beside her and pull her into his arms?

She smiled and closed the book. She shook her hands briefly, like she was getting circulation back into them. Looked like she'd been writing for way too long.

"This is nice," she said, leaning back against the tree. "I thought I'd want to be on the go all the time, but it does feel good to relax after being on the road all day."

He nodded. "Yeah, it does."

She looked around them. "I hardly even notice all the people at the other sites."

The campground was nearly full, sites occupied by colorful tents, huge motorhomes and everything in between. Kids on bikes zipped around the narrow roads. Older couples strolled by, many walking small dogs on leashes.

He and Sarah could have been the only people in the campground, as far as Dean was concerned. He'd been pretty much focused on her since they set up camp. He had to find a way to get his mind off of her and her shiny hair and wet lips.

"I've always liked it better outside," Dean said, responding to Sarah's comment instead of her lips. "No walls around me. Ever since I was a kid."

"Oh, is that why..." she broke off.

"Why what?"

She hesitated. "I was going to ask if that's why you hung out on the streets?"

She didn't need to know the real reason why. "Yeah, well, we didn't actually have a lot of open spaces to roam in the neighborhood."

"That must be why you like to ride a motorcycle more than a car."

Was that why? He shrugged. "I guess so. I never thought about it."

"The fire's nice," she said and stretched her arms above her head. Dean tried not to stare at the way her T-shirt pulled enticingly across her breasts. She took off her sunglasses and placed them and the journal on the grass beside her. "So tell me about your job."

"My job?"

"Yeah. Working for a rock band, traveling all over the world sounds pretty exciting for someone who's been stuck in a bank in Buffalo for the past eight years."

Dean sighed and stared into the fire. The flames leapt and danced, laughing at him. She wouldn't want the truth. It wouldn't play well with his rebel image and the excitement she wanted on this trip. She wanted to think she'd skipped town with the bad boy.

But he didn't like lying to her.

He glanced back at Sarah and saw her waiting patiently, her eyes bright in the gathering darkness. The leaping flames threw flickering shadows against her face. He looked back at the fire.

"It's just a job," he said softly.

"Oh, come on. Are there wild parties every night? Girls hanging around the stage doors?"

"The sound crew doesn't hang out with the musicians," Dean said. He kept his eyes trained on the hot coals deep within the fire. He couldn't look her in the face. "We set the equipment up before the show, then tear it down afterward. Any girls hanging around are waiting for the band. They would be long gone before we ever finished."

"Too bad for you," she said, a smile in her voice.

He looked up and saw the real thing on her face. He smiled back. "Nah, I'm always exhausted by the time I'm done. I'm off to bed. Not the wild and exciting life you thought, huh?"

"Sure it is. Compared to cashing checks all day in the same place."

"There's something to be said for staying in one place, Sarah."

"Yeah, it's boring. It's stifling. It gets a stranglehold on your life and by the time you realize you've been choked, it's too late."

She gasped softly and looked away from him, as if she couldn't believe she said those things out loud. Her face was in shadows now. The desperation was back in her voice.

"Is there something you want to talk about?" Dean asked. "I'm a good listener."

She was silent for a moment. "No, I'm fine," she said finally, her voice sounding forcibly upbeat. "I don't know why I said all that. I have no reason to have said all that. Don't pay any attention to me. I'm tired, I guess."

Dean frowned. He'd heard that fake cheeriness more times than he could count. He wished she'd tell him what was bothering her, but he knew from experience that trying to force the issue would simply make her clam up tighter.

"So, Dean, got some special girl waiting for you at one of your ports of call?" Her voice was soft again, almost tentative.

"All women are special as far as I'm concerned," he said. "But only one? Not a chance."

"Yeah, that's what I thought. Same old Dean. Did you know they called you Love 'em and Leave 'em Bastian back in high school?"

He winced at the reminder. It may have been true—hell, it *still* was true—but that didn't mean he liked the name. It implied some callousness on his part, and he'd always been very careful about the women he got involved with, even in high school. He'd parted friends with every one of them. They usually ended up feeling sorry for him because he had a character flaw that made him unable to get serious about any one woman.

"Yeah, I knew that, but I didn't know you knew that."

"Oh, sure I did." But there wasn't sarcasm or disgust in her voice like he thought there might be. If he didn't know better, there seemed to be a touch of affection in her voice. She gathered up her book and sunglasses and started to stand up. She groaned and wobbled a little, leaning back against the tree. After she dropped what she was holding, she grabbed her butt and slid back down to the ground.

"Are you okay?" he asked.

"You may be used to sitting on that bike all day, but I'm not. I'm a long way from having an iron butt."

He chuckled lightly. "You'll get used to it." Then before he could think about all the reasons he shouldn't, he said, "Lie down on your stomach."

She looked up at him and frowned. "What?"

"Lie down on your stomach," he repeated. He knew he would regret doing this, but he'd already knelt beside her. "I think a massage is in order."

Her eyes widened. "You're going to massage my butt?"

"Do you want to feel better or not?"

"Oh, yeah." She grinned. "I just wanted to make sure that's really what you had in mind."

He knew he was in deep trouble, but he made himself smile back. He took the sleeping bag she'd been sitting on and spread it out beneath the tree. She lay down on her stomach, her denim-clad legs and bottom stretching out beside him. She cradled her head on her arms and looked back at him.

"Okay. I'm ready."

Dean was glad for the darkness that finally enveloped their campsite. The campfire light flickered over them. His heart beat in a matching, uneven rhythm. He flexed his fingers and imagined touching her. He reached out his hands and held them in the air, suspended over her tight buns. What did he think he was doing? How could he touch her there, of all places, and not want to touch her everywhere else?

And how could he not want to make love with her before they were done?

Hell, wanting had never been the problem. Controlling that desire was where he had his difficulty.

"Dean?"

She was still lying there, willing to submit to his attention. Trusting him to make her feel better. He was simply going to massage her sore and tired muscles. That's all. He could do this. And to prove it to himself, he lowered his hands to the shapely denim.

Soft, yet firm. Hard, yet yielding. Dean rubbed and kneaded the knotted muscles and tried to put sweet little Sarah out of his mind. He was simply massaging some aching muscles. He was giving aid where it was needed.

He was so hard it hurt.

Sarah moaned and shimmied closer to him. "Oh, yes," she murmured. "Yes, right there. Oh, that feels incredible."

He swallowed and shifted position to try to relieve some of the pressure on his zipper. She was killing him, but he kept it up, massaging the tense muscles in her thighs and buttocks. He tried to focus his attention on his hands and watch them rather than looking at Sarah.

What a joke. From the glow of the fire he could see her. Not the details, not the little things that didn't matter right now, but her shapely body as a whole. The way her hips curved out just enough to make them hips, a woman's hips. The way her waist narrowed and her shoulders gracefully broadened, supporting the slender neck that he could admire now that her hair was short. And her ears, so delicate, and though he couldn't see them now, he could picture the little gold balls he'd noticed earlier decorating the lobes.

"Um, Dean?"

Sarah's voice brought him back from his musings about her body. He noticed that his massaging strokes had slowed down and deteriorated into something more like a grope. He snatched his hands away.

"Sorry."

She sat up close beside him, too close. "That's okay," she said. "Thank you. That was wonderful. I feel a lot better."

She looked at him for a moment, as if she expected him to say something or do something. He wished he knew what she was thinking and what she wanted him to do.

"Well, I think I'm going to turn in," she said finally, her voice soft, almost seductive. She picked up her journal and the sunglasses. "You coming?"

That certainly sounded seductive. Dean looked at the little tent. What had he been thinking? There was no way he was crawling in there with her now. He'd never be able to sleep lying close enough to her that their breaths would mingle in the darkness. How would he ever avoid touching her, smelling her, pulling her into his arms and burying his body deep inside hers?

He jumped to his feet. "I'm going to sleep out here." He picked up the second sleeping bag and spread it out on the other side of the campfire.

She slowly got to her feet and walked over to him. She placed her hand on his arm. It felt as if a spark from the fire had landed there. "What if it rains tonight? There's plenty of room in the tent for both of us."

He looked up at the darkened sky. Bright stars twinkled through the smattering of clouds. "It's not going to rain," he said. "I told you I like to be outdoors. I always sleep in the fresh air. I only brought the tent along for you to sleep in."

Without warning, she reached out and brushed a hand as soft as velvet across his cheek. A smile slowly spread across her face. "Do I make you nervous, Dean?"

Her eyes glowed from the reflection of the flames. He wished he could lie to her, pretend he was unaffected by her being there, only a heartbeat away. But he'd already told her too many lies.

Smoke from the campfire swirled around them, making it hard for him to breathe. "You make me real nervous, Sarah," he replied. Why did his voice suddenly sound so ragged? It must have been the smoke.

She leaned forward and brushed her lips lightly across his. "I liked kissing you," she whispered, her lips moving against his. "Kiss me again, Dean."

Hell, he was only human. He gathered her into his arms and leaned in to claim her lips without a second thought. She was eager, nibbling first his top lip, then his bottom, drawing it into her mouth. He moaned and brought her down with him onto his sleeping bag. Sitting there, he gathered her closer still, bringing her softness nearer to him.

Was this little Sarah Austin who turned his blood to liquid fire? Sarah, who was innocent and good? Sarah, who he promised himself he wouldn't take advantage of?

But who was taking advantage of whom? She had crawled into his lap. Her hands roamed over his neck and back. She rained kisses over his face, her lips smooth and moist. Her soft breasts pressed against his chest. Her firm thighs straddled one of his.

He cupped her face in his hands and captured Sarah's mouth, that teasing, tantalizing mouth, with his own. She tasted like spearmint and sin, tempting him to go where he'd vowed he wouldn't go. She opened her mouth to him and he dove in, stroking the soft recesses with his tongue as desire coursed through his body.

The fire crackled behind him, children laughed and a dog barked somewhere nearby. But those sounds were filtered through the passion pounding his heart, pulsing his blood. One of his hands found its way under her shirt. Her skin was soft and warm beneath his fingers. He caught the cup of her bra with his thumb and lifted it, so that he could hold the exquisite weight of her breast in his hands. He kneaded it lightly and then rolled the pebbly nipple beneath his thumb.

Sarah moaned and wriggled against him, rocking slightly back and forth on his leg. "Please, Dean, please," she murmured softly, her breath warm against his face.

He knew that itch. Knew what she longed for. He was experiencing the same desire. Hell, his arousal pulsed with need. His entire body was one giant itch. How much longer was his mind going to have any say over the need rushing through his body? How long before they dashed into the tent, tore their clothes off, and satisfied that overwhelming need?

What kind of man would he be if he gave into temptation his first night out? What kind of man would he be if he broke his own vow?

He would be a weak man. A weak man like his father, who gave into his desires for booze and women without a second thought to anything else but his own sorry itches.

Dean had worked his whole life *not* to turn out like his father.

His body cried out in frustration as he let go of that marvelous breast and straightened the bra back over it. He slid his hand out from under her shirt and reluctantly broke away from the mind-blowing kiss. He let go of her and leaned back, away from the warmth of her body.

Sarah slowly opened her eyes and gazed at him in confusion. What was happening? Where did Dean go? They had been in the middle of the most awesome kiss she'd ever had in her whole life. Her entire body buzzed with the need to make love with this man.

She looked at his face through the waning haze of passion, unable to read his expression in the darkness. Something was terribly wrong. Her whole body went from burning with passion to burning with embarrassment. She slid off his leg and landed on the hard ground. She lifted her chin and looked away from him. Her eyes filled with tears but she refused to let them spill down her cheeks.

Dean stood up and stepped away from her. "I'm sorry, Sarah," he said, his voice smooth. "I shouldn't have let that get out of hand."

If he could play it cool, so could she. She cleared her throat and hoped the disappointment wouldn't show in her voice. "Oh, I don't know. I thought you had things pretty well *in* hand."

He laughed lightly, but she almost thought she heard sadness there as well. "Good night, Sarah."

She scrambled to her feet as quickly as she was able and walked back over to her sleeping bag. She dragged it up into her arms and turned to the tent. She tripped slightly in her rush to get inside. Things weren't going at all the way she had planned. After she'd zipped herself up in the tent, she sat down on the sleeping bag and pulled her knees up to her chest, hugging them against her.

She was scared. She'd tried not to think about the illness she had. The incurable illness. Her future was one big question mark. The very real possibility of her becoming severely disabled threatened to paralyze her with fear whenever it popped into her mind.

She'd told herself she wasn't going to think about it now. But that was easier said than done. The only way she could function was to focus on this trip. Focus on the adventure. And the memories.

This was her one chance to make memories to last the rest of her life. If Dean didn't want to love her and leave her, she was going to have to find a way to change his mind.

Chapter Five

Sarah tossed and turned in the tiny tent. Her body was restless and her brain wouldn't shut down.

Images of Dean, lying a few feet away in the cool night air, wove in and out of her brain. Blissful memories of his hands on her body, massaging her tight muscles, nearly made her moan out loud. Thoughts of his mouth and what it could do to her...well, no wonder she was restless.

She couldn't get over the way he made her feel. The teenage crush she had on Dean was over years ago. They had only met again yesterday. How could she feel this burning inside? She'd never felt like this about any of the other guys she'd dated. It didn't make any sense.

Sarah turned over again, burying her face in the sleeping bag. Besides, Dean didn't want her. Well, he was a guy, of course he *wanted* her. But for some reason, he didn't want to give into the urge with her.

He couldn't have made it any clearer. He was just doing her a favor. He was giving her a ride. She had to face it. That's all this trip was to him.

If only...

No!

Sarah flopped over onto her back. There was no room in her life for "if only." She didn't *want* anything with Dean to be special. She wanted it to be physical. Okay, maybe she wanted it to be mind-blowing. She certainly wanted it to be memorable. But that's all she wanted.

That was all she could have.

Sarah would have sworn she'd never fallen asleep, but then there was the dream. Funny how she knew it was a dream even when it started. It seemed so real. She could smell the lilacs on the bush in front of Mrs. Cheney's porch. She heard the lawnmower in the yard next door. She saw the sunlight glint off the chrome on Mrs. Cheney's wheelchair.

Mrs. Cheney had been her favorite teacher. But throughout Sarah's fourth-grade year, her teacher had gotten sicker and sicker. The term MS was whispered, but Sarah and her friends didn't know what it meant. The first day she'd had to bring a cane to school so she didn't stumble so much, Mrs. Cheney had explained to the class that a monster was attacking the nerves in her body and soon she wouldn't be able to walk. Soon she wouldn't be able to teach.

Everyone had cried and Mrs. Cheney had taught through the end of the school year. But she didn't come back in the fall. Sarah's mother had taken Sarah to see her the following spring. Sarah remembered Mrs. Cheney sitting on her front porch and that's where the dream started.

Sarah was alone in the dream, though. Her mother wasn't there this time to squeeze her hand and smooth over the conversation. Sarah walked slowly up the brick walk, stopping at the bottom of the porch steps. The steps seemed to stretch out higher than she remembered. Mrs. Cheney looked thinner, almost frail, in a floral dress and the ugly wheelchair. Sarah's heart beat in her chest, painfully hard, like a fist pounding against her ribs. Mrs. Cheney smiled at her, but Sarah's lips trembled when she tried to return the smile.

Mrs. Cheney had a plate of chocolate chip cookies on the table beside her and she invited Sarah up onto the porch with her. Sarah was frozen in place. She didn't want to go up there. She wanted to turn and head for home as fast as she could.

"You can't run away," Mrs. Cheney said, her voice low and eerie in this dream world. She rolled her wheelchair to the top of the steps and loomed large in front of Sarah. "This will be your world soon."

Sarah shook her head frantically. Her mind screamed but she couldn't force any sound out from her clenched jaws.

"Come, Sarah. Come here with me." Mrs. Cheney stretched out her arms and Sarah took a step away. "You'll be like me soon, Sarah. Soon."

Suddenly Sarah was on the porch, standing behind the wheelchair. Dreams didn't require legs to carry you up the stairs. Dreams plopped you wherever they wanted you to be. The porch began to whirl around her, as if she were in the middle of a merry-go-round. The table with the cookies, the wheelchair, the door to the house, all of them spun around her. Sarah wrapped her arms around her, willing herself to stand still, to not let the dizziness overcome her. The word "soon" echoed around her, screeching from all directions.

As quickly as it started to whirl, the spinning ceased. The wheelchair stopped in front of her. But it wasn't Mrs. Cheney sitting there in the floral dress and the shining chrome.

It was Sarah.

She woke up with a start, her scream echoing in her ears. A cold sweat poured over her. She sat up, drew her knees to her chest, and wrapped her trembling arms around them.

Her subconscious had been reminding her of the reality

waiting for her. This was the life she had ahead of her. Sitting on the porch, watching life go by.

"Sarah?"

She heard Dean's concerned voice a second before the sound of the tent's zipper raising. Her heart hadn't stopped pounding yet from the aftereffects of the dream, but it kicked into overdrive when he pushed his way into the tent.

"Are you okay?"

"I'm fine." She knew she didn't sound fine. Her voice wavered, even on those two small words. She was still shaking, still breathless, still terrified of the future.

"I heard you scream." He crawled up beside her in the tiny tent and put his arm around her. "You're shaking."

"Bad dream," she mumbled and curled into him. He wasn't wearing a shirt and she sighed as she rested her cheek on his bare shoulder. "Hold me for a minute?"

"Of course." He pulled her closer. She felt his blue jeans rub against her bare legs and wondered if he'd slept with them on or grabbed them before he came to her.

She breathed him in. He smelled like campfire and fresh air and a musky scent that was all Dean. His skin was warm, his breathing deep, and while his embrace should have relaxed her, a little buzz of arousal began to grow inside her. Here she was, in Dean's arms, right where she wanted to be.

She didn't think first when she dropped a kiss onto his shoulder. She felt his quick intake of breath, heard the soft gasp, but he didn't stop her, so she did it again, a little lower this time, on his hard nipple. His heart thudded beneath her ear. She ran her hand over him in the darkness. His soft hair. Muscled chest. Unsnapped jeans. Hard erection.

"Sarah..." He started to pull away.

"I don't want forever, Dean," she said quickly, softly, because she didn't know how far their voices would carry in the quiet of the night. She cupped his face in her hands. "I know that's not your style." She leaned forward and ran her tongue along his lips. "I won't ask for more after this trip is over. You have my word on that." She licked him again, more brazen than she'd ever been in her life. "I just want you." She brushed his crotch again with her hand. "Now."

He groaned and pulled her onto his lap, straddling his hips. "I promised myself I wouldn't do this."

His erection was thick between her legs. It was impossible not to rock against him. Desire shot through her, combined with worry for his hesitation. "Why not?"

His strangled laughter was mixed with another groan. "I didn't want to take advantage of you."

Relieved laughter bubbled out of her and she ran her hands over his muscled arms. "I don't think you have to worry about that."

"But I'm not a settling-down kind of guy. And you're not the kind of girl who'd be happy with a quick fling."

Now that she'd started touching him, she couldn't stop. She combed her fingers through his hair, rubbing the silky strands between her fingertips. She wanted to rub him everywhere. "I'll be happy. Honest."

Dean caught her hands and brought them down to her sides. "I'm serious, Sarah. Happily ever after isn't in the cards for me. If we have sex now—"

"If we have sex now," Sarah interrupted, "think of all the great memories we'll have of this trip."

He slid his hands under the oversized T-shirt she slept in. His fingers skimmed over her, sending delicious shivers along her skin. "You're making it hard to resist you."

73

She stripped the shirt from her body. She was completely naked underneath. "So don't resist."

Dean reached out and gathered her breasts in his hands. She arched her back and threw her head back. Oh yes, this was what she wanted—more of what he'd teased her with earlier, more of these incredible sensations. He skimmed his thumbs across her nipples, sending tingles of desire washing over her.

Slamming into her was more like it. She grabbed onto his shoulders and captured his lips with hers. He tasted like all the forbidden fantasies she'd dreamed of but never dared make real. She drank him in, drank in the courage, the passion. And, all the while, desire built within her.

He tore his mouth away, breathing heavily. "You're killing me."

"What?"

He pushed her back so she wasn't sitting on his erection. "Much more of that wriggling and I'll be shooting off in my jeans like a teenager."

"Sorry." She didn't even realize she'd been moving like that. "Guess we better take care of this zipper then." She grabbed the tab.

He put his hand over hers. "Easy."

She chuckled. "Oops. Sorry again." She slid the zipper down slowly and discovered that he wasn't wearing boxers or briefs beneath the denim. His stiff erection sprang free and bounced against her hand.

It was too dark to see much more than shapes and shadows. She took him in her hands and gently ran her hands over the hot skin. He was long and thick, soft and hard at the same time. Veins bulged on the underside. The round head was smooth and warm.

She inched forward so that his hard flesh rubbed against the sensitive spot between her legs. She'd grown wet and he slid easily through her slippery folds. Her heart skipped like crazy, her breath came in quick pants. She wasn't going to last long either. She needed to feel him inside her first.

"Wait," he groaned when she rose above him. "Condom. Back pocket." He lifted a little onto his knees and pulled it out, then ripped it open and rolled it on. She guessed he wasn't going to last any longer than she was.

Sarah grabbed onto his shoulders with one hand and, with the other, guided him into her. He slid in smoothly, stretching her, filling her. She moved up and down along his length. Her head bumped against the top of the dome tent, but she didn't care. Her legs would probably rebel sooner or later, but right now nothing felt as great as Dean deep inside her.

He grabbed onto her ass as she rode him hard. She liked the feel of him holding on to her. They were both slick with sweat as they moved together. He rocked his hips too as he thrust into her, angling the slide so that he brushed against her clit with each stroke. The need swirled within her, rising higher, building stronger until it exploded into a burst of indescribable sensations.

She screamed when she came, burying the sound in his shoulder. He followed her a few strokes later, his stifled groans music to her ears. They collapsed, panting, onto the sleeping bag.

They did it. They really did it. Sex with Dean was as wonderful as Sarah imagined it would be. Already she wished they could have more than just a few days together. But she knew it did no good to wish. She promised Dean she'd be happy with a quick fling. And she would.

She'd have to.

Later, as they lay side by side, Dean kissed her on the tip of her nose and asked, "No regrets?"

She had a lot of regrets, but none about what they'd done tonight. She rolled into his embrace and answered, "No regrets."

🏍 🏍 🏍

The morning-after awkwardness Dean feared never happened. They slept in each other's arms and Sarah woke him with a kiss and a smile.

"Don't get up," she said softly. "I'm going to get my shower in before the bathhouse fills up." She moaned a little as she turned away from him.

Dean rose up on his elbows and studied her through sleep-fogged eyes. "Are you all right?"

"My hips got a workout last night," she said as she pulled clean clothes out of her bag. She flashed him a grin. "I'm not used to being on top."

"I'll be on top tonight."

She was at the door of the tent and he had an enticing view of her shapely ass. She glanced at him over her shoulder. "I think I like it on top."

Dean smiled and plopped back down on the sleeping bag. "Go get your shower. We have to get a lot of miles in today."

"Don't forget we stay off the expressway today." She dropped the tent flap behind her as she left.

He closed his eyes and didn't question the smile that lifted his lips.

They didn't get fifty miles down the road before Sarah bounced on the seat behind him and pointed to a sign for a small town summer festival. Dean rolled his eyes, but turned off at the bright red arrow and found a parking space behind an old-fashioned hardware store.

"How did we get so lucky?" Sarah asked as they walked down the short main street. "A summer festival. It doesn't get any better than this."

Dean shrugged. If he'd been by himself, he would have blown by this place without a second thought. He'd certainly never go out of his way to attend a small-town festival. But he had to admit there was something appealing about walking down the quaint street with Sarah that suddenly made it a pleasant way to spend a few hours. Her legs seemed to be a little stiff from riding, so it was good to walk around for a while anyway.

They grabbed some hot dogs and sodas from a street vendor and made a path to the town square. All the benches were full, so they sat on the grass beneath a spreading maple tree. A barbershop quartet sang in the white gazebo in the middle of the square.

"Isn't that harmony beautiful?" Sarah asked with a sigh. She ran her hand, almost absently, along his arm. "Wow, that last chord gave me goose bumps."

"I guess," Dean said. Watching Sarah gave *him* goose bumps. Her gentle touch did too. He'd never thought cute and sexy would go together, but they were a perfect blend in Sarah. He had a hard time taking his eyes off her, with her pixie hairdo and her tight, gold tank top with the deep "V" neckline. He swallowed hard as he looked at the long stretch of bare skin that ran from jaw line to cleavage. Now that he'd had his hands on that soft skin, his fingers itched to do it again. Dean hungered for more than a hot dog.

Sarah ate her hot dog with enthusiasm. Ketchup and

mustard squirted out of her mouth and dribbled down her chin. He reached out with a napkin to wipe it up before she wore it on her shirt.

She laughed. "Thanks." She set the rest of the hot dog down on the napkin in her lap and sighed. "Isn't this a perfect day? Not too sunny, not too cloudy. Nothing pressing to do. Just a lazy afternoon."

She looked over his shoulder and suddenly got a wistful expression on her face.

Dean turned his head, curious as to what she saw. There were dozens of people milling around the square, but a family crossing in front of them caught his attention. The mother pushed a colorful stroller that carried a little girl holding the string of a big red balloon. The father carried a laughing little boy on his shoulders.

An unexpected longing punched Dean in the gut, shocking him with its intensity. What was he thinking? One look at Sarah told him she wanted to have a family of her own, but a family like that could never be part of his future.

He laughed bitterly to himself. Sarah obviously realized that too. While she only wanted to have sex with him, she still wanted a family.

Just not with him.

He couldn't blame her. After all, what did he know about raising a family? His childhood nights had been more often than not spent hiding under the covers while he held his stomach and listened to his parents scream and throw things. He'd never ridden on his father's shoulders. Or laughed at a colorful balloon.

He watched the mother and father exchange glances, a secret look meant only for each other. They looked happy together. How did they do it? How did anyone find someone they could be happy with for the rest of their lives? He was deathly afraid he'd wake up one day married to a woman he didn't love because he got her pregnant, and then resent it for the rest of his life.

Dean leapt to his feet. These weren't memories he needed to dredge up right now. He hadn't turned out like his father, but he still lived with the fear that it could happen any time. Would he ever be free from it?

Sarah looked up at him, confusion on her face. "What's wrong?"

He wanted to jump on his bike and ride as fast as he could. Ride until the wind had blown all those thoughts from his mind. But he was here with Sarah and, after a moment, he realized this was where he wanted to be. "I'm still hungry. Want another hot dog?"

She shook her head. "No, but if you run across candy apples, could you bring me back one?"

He smiled and bowed slightly, "Your wish is my command." Then he laughed and walked away.

What would Dean do if he knew what she really wished for? Sarah watched him walk away from her, his tight buns shifting seductively in his blue jeans. Boy, she wished she could get her hands on those right now. She laughed to herself at the wishes going through her mind.

She wished for more nights making love with Dean. More nights riding him hard and loving him harder. More nights holding each other close.

Sarah's breath caught in her chest. She wished she could have a future with him. She wished she could have children with him and bring them to the park and run and play with them.

She stuffed the rest of her hot dog in her mouth to stop the cry that wanted to escape. Who was she kidding? Even if she didn't have MS haunting her, she knew Dean wasn't interested in that kind of future. He'd made that clear. He wasn't a wife and kiddies kind of guy. He liked to be on his own, not concerned with anyone's wishes but his own.

She reminded herself that this was exactly how she had wanted it to be too. How she wanted him to be. But it didn't make her mourn any less for what could never be.

She stood up when she saw him walk toward her, a half-eaten hot dog in one hand and a candy apple in the other. The lines in his face had relaxed some today. The smile he sent her when he caught her eye sent tingles of delight along her skin. She knew she would never get tired of looking at him.

How could she have forgotten a camera? Maybe she should buy a disposable one and take some pictures of Dean to keep with her journal. He popped the last of the hot dog in his mouth as he stopped in front of her. Her mouth watered, and it wasn't over the apple.

Forget the camera. She didn't need a picture to remind her how it felt to make love with Dean. How his lips sent shivers along her skin. How his hands teased all sorts of sensations from her eager body. How his body wrapped around hers in the dark hours of the night. She didn't need any more reminders of what she couldn't keep. "Okay, I'm ready to go whenever you are."

He handed her the plastic-wrapped candy apple and frowned slightly. "Are you sure? I thought you wanted to do some shopping." He swept his arm around the square. "Look at all these booths."

Sarah shook her head. "No, that's okay. We should be going. I don't need to do any shopping."

Dean ignored her babbling and took her hand in his. They started walking toward the line of vendors. She didn't want to think about how good her hand felt in his. She felt warm and safe and aroused all at the same time.

"Oh, come on," Dean said as they browsed the line of tables. "Don't you want a stuffed monkey? Or a copper bracelet? Or a...what is this?"

They'd stopped in front of a table packed with items made out of plastic canvas and decorated with colorful yarns. Dean picked up a square pink box and slid his hand from the open bottom through a hole in the top.

Sarah laughed. "That's a tissue holder."

"Really?" Dean took his hand out and set it back down on the table. He smiled at the woman looking expectantly at them from behind the table. "It's very nice, but I'm afraid it won't fit in my saddlebag."

The woman smiled and nodded, but obviously had no idea what Dean was talking about.

"Did you make these all yourself?" Dean asked her.

"Oh, yes," the gray-haired woman replied, a look of pride on her face. "I stitch all winter long so I can sell them in the summer."

"Well, it's beautiful handiwork," Dean said. He winked at her and the woman giggled and blushed.

Dean picked up a blue and white bookmark. "Now this I have room for," he said. He looked at Sarah. "Do you want one too? My treat."

"Sure," she said with a smile. "I'll take the rainbow one."

After Dean had paid for their purchases and they strolled by the next few tables, Sarah put her hand on his arm.

He stopped and looked at her. "What?"

"I never thought you'd be the type of guy to buy some tacky bookmarks and flirt with little old ladies."

His expression seemed to shut down for a split second, then he flashed a cocky grin. "That's right, bad boys don't do nice things, do they?"

"That's not what I mean and you know it." She studied him for a moment, trying to figure out how to explain what she meant without sounding judgmental or mean-spirited. The longer she was with Dean, the more she learned that he wasn't just the hunk with the bad reputation she knew from the old neighborhood. In fact, she wasn't seeing much of the old Dean at all.

Or maybe she never really knew that Dean.

Dean shrugged and went on before she had a chance to say anything else. "Even a lone rebel can realize that the poor woman worked real hard on those ugly things and no one was buying any."

"I know. Somehow I was afraid you wouldn't be comfortable in small-town surroundings like this." Sarah reached up and wiped a spot of mustard off the edge of his mouth. "I never realized you were such a big softy."

"Me? Don't you believe it." But the sparkle in his eye told her otherwise. And Sarah realized she shouldn't have been surprised. After all, it was Dean who always rescued her when the neighborhood bullies tried to pick on her. Jimmy Clark's nose was never the same after Dean punched him for stealing her lunch.

Sarah hadn't even realized her hand was still up by his face. She loved his face. She swept her fingers across his cheek and down his jaw. Softness and roughness both played against her fingertips causing delicious shivers to ripple through her.

What was she doing? They were in the middle of a public

park. She had to put some distance between herself and temptation. She couldn't rub up against him here the way she wanted to. But when she started to pull away, Dean captured her hand with his and held it there to the side of his face. He turned his face, so that his lips pressed into her palm. Then suddenly the tip of his tongue tickled the sensitive skin. More shivers flowed over her.

Sarah took a step closer to him. Maybe she could make some more unforgettable memories with Dean. She moved closer yet, molding her body into his. The candy apple fell to the ground as she wrapped her other arm around his waist. His hard thighs pressed against hers. She could feel the heat from his body seeping into hers, warming her blood, quickening her pulse.

The world around them faded into a haze. The din of dozens of conversations became a low buzz. She caught Dean's heated gaze and wondered how she'd never before noticed the flecks of gold mixed in with the brown of his eyes.

There were a lot of things she'd never noticed about Dean before. She didn't know why the thought was so disconcerting. What else didn't she know about him? Who was this man she was as close as sin with?

Looking into his eyes, it didn't matter. Instead of being disturbing, it was intriguing to think about all the other little things she might learn about Dean on this trip. She couldn't help but wonder what else there was to discover about him.

Like would the next kiss between them be as powerful as the last?

She was about to rise up on tiptoes to find out, when she felt a tap on her arm. She blinked and looked down to see a little boy with tousled hair and a toothy grin holding her candy apple.

"Lady, you dropped this."

She smiled sheepishly and stepped away from Dean. She glanced up at him and he grinned. She took the apple from the little boy. "Thank you so much."

The boy smiled and looked up at Dean. "Mister?"

"Yes?"

"Were you gonna *kiss* her?" The little towhead wrinkled his nose as if to say what he thought about that.

"Uh, yeah, I was thinking about it," Dean said. He glanced at Sarah and then back down at the little boy. "What do you think?"

The boy shook his head emphatically. "I don't like kissing. Do you?"

Dean looked at Sarah once more and she felt herself grow warm again under his gaze. "Yeah, believe it or not, I do."

"Oh, well, go ahead if you like to do it. I'm not gonna do it, though." The boy's mother called him and he turned and ran off with a wave.

Dean laughed and turned back to Sarah. He pulled her into his arms. "Well, as long as I was given the go ahead."

His lips were hot and wet as they swept along hers. He tasted of spicy mustard and sweet relish. She drank him in greedily but, oh, so briefly. Dean was obviously as aware as she was that they were standing in the town square surrounded by dozens of people. He slowly pulled away from her, landing a brief kiss on her nose before stepping away.

"You want to do any more shopping?" he asked.

She shook her head. She wanted to get on to the next campground. She had plans for tonight.

"Let's get on the road."

As they covered mile after mile, Dean couldn't help but think about Sarah's comments about the type of guy she thought he was. She seemed to accept without question that he was still the bad boy she knew in school. He'd tried, but Dean knew he wasn't playing the part true to form. He simply wasn't that guy anymore and it wasn't as easy as he thought it would be to slip back into his skin.

He didn't like lying to her. He'd told himself it was what she wanted. She wanted an adventure, and part of that adventure was running off with the rebel biker. She'd be disappointed to find out his life now was as simple as hers was.

What would Sarah say if she found out about the counseling service he worked for? That he drew from his own background to help troubled teens work out their issues? He liked to think she'd be proud of him. Growing up, everyone in the neighborhood, especially his father, predicted Dean would end up a no-good bum, on the wrong side of the law.

Dean had been determined to prove them all wrong. He found himself wishing he could tell Sarah about it. He wanted to tell her how he'd worked his way through college and about the advisor there who'd steered him toward counseling. He wanted to let her know how much satisfaction he got from his work.

He wanted to tell her about the kids.

About Rico, a kid from a family so much like Dean's it was scary, and how Dean worked with him for two years to get him through high school and accepted into college. About Heather, who was now taking the generous allowance she used to blow on drugs and saving it to buy a Harley of her own.

Dean couldn't have been prouder of them if they had been his own kids. He found himself foolishly sad that he couldn't share that with Sarah.

They stopped at a gas station at the edge of yet another little town, filled the gas tank, and used the restrooms. When they were ready to head out again, Dean said, "We need to be looking out for campground signs now. The clerk inside said there's a couple coming up. We want to set up camp before it gets dark."

Sarah nodded. "Okay." She rubbed her hip against his. "I'm looking forward to it."

His jeans felt tighter just from thinking about the promise in her voice. She had her leather jacket on and her helmet in her hand. She looked like a model for a bike magazine. She should be one. He'd buy any bike or accessory she was selling.

They weren't out of town more than five or ten minutes when Sarah poked his shoulder. He didn't see any campground signs, but he slowed the bike and pulled over to the side of the road.

"What is it?" he asked.

She flipped up the visor on her helmet. Her eyes were bright. "What's that?" she asked, pointing to the right.

Dean turned to look in that direction and saw her point at a long, low building sitting back off the road with a number of motorcycles parked outside. The gray siding needed painting and the windows were dingy. Not quite a dive, but not too far up the ladder. What had gotten into that mind of hers now? "It's just a bar."

"A biker bar?" she asked, like it was the most exciting thing in the world.

"Yeah, I suppose."

"Let's go in!"

She started to hop off the bike and he grabbed her arm. "Sarah, I'm not taking you into a biker bar."

She frowned and pulled her arm away. "Why not? We're bikers, aren't we?"

Dean sighed. "Sarah, let's go. We have to set up camp before it gets dark."

"But you said that today I could pick where we stopped."

Now she was pouting. He wanted to suck that wet lower lip into his mouth and take her mind off seedy bars.

"Sarah, we don't know what kind of people are in there. I mean, I'm sure they'll be fine, but there's always a chance this is one of those bars where the patrons don't look favorably on strangers coming into their place."

Sarah climbed off the bike and moved away from it before he could stop her. "I'm going in," she said. She turned and walked away from him without a backward glance.

Dean cursed. He was already well past the drive into the place. He revved the engine to begin a U-turn in the road. His mind on Sarah, he nearly pulled into the path of a dusty orange dump truck. His heart hammered in his chest as it rumbled by him, close enough to try to suck him into its wake.

He cursed even louder and told himself to get his mind off Sarah. But he turned to see her cross the ditch and head for the bar. With a quick glance to check for oncoming traffic, he headed after her. He hoped she didn't get into any trouble before he caught up with her.

Chapter Six

Sarah stumbled a bit crossing the ditch, then tried not to limp as she crossed the grass to the parking lot. She yanked the helmet off her head.

What was she thinking? What made her hop off the motorcycle and head for the long, low building with a neon sign that read Pitt's Stop? Every instinct in her body cried for her to turn around and go back to Dean. But still she kept walking.

Her right foot seemed to drag a little bit. Probably because she was tired. Maybe because she'd walked so much today. Or maybe because she screwed too much last night. Or was she losing control of her foot permanently? The thought dropped a rock into the pit of her stomach.

She could only guess at the reason. All the information the neurologist had given her last week was stuffed in a desk drawer in her living room. She hadn't read a word of it. Somehow, at the time, reading about it would have made it true.

And she didn't want it to be true.

Don't think about it now, she told herself. She concentrated on walking smoothly, adding a little hip wiggle for Dean's benefit. The helmet bounced off her thigh. Maybe he wouldn't notice the limp.

When she'd come home from the doctor's office, she'd seen no sense in reading about all the terrible things that could happen to her. She just wasn't ready for that yet. What difference would it make anyway? What was going to happen to her body would happen.

Besides, she already knew what MS could do.

This was why she'd hopped off the bike. Why she wanted to go into that bar. All too soon she would be at the mercy of the disease. Her life was never going to be the same again. When she was sitting on her porch, watching the rest of the world go by, she didn't want to wonder forever what it was like inside a biker bar.

She wanted to know.

Dean caught up with her before she got to the front door. He grabbed her arm. "Wait, Sarah."

She spun around and yanked her arm from his gentle grasp. "I'm thirsty, Dean." Her voice sounded tired, even to her own ears. "I want to get something to drink. If you don't want to go in, it's okay."

He took a step back. She couldn't blame him for the confusion on his face. "What? You want me to wait out here in the parking lot for you?"

"Yes. No. I don't know." She was too tired for all this banter. Why did he have to make it so complicated? "I just want to see it, Dean. I just need a few minutes."

"Okay, Sarah. I wasn't going to try to talk you out of it again. I noticed you were limping and wanted to make sure you were okay."

"Oh, I'm sorry." So much for the hip wiggle distracting him. "I'm okay. Really. I guess my foot fell asleep." Her foot kind of felt like that, but the pins and needles sensation was even more intense. She knew she should forget about this, go on to the

89

campground and get some rest, but she didn't want to live with any regrets.

And right now she regretted the way she'd talked to Dean. She smiled up at him and threaded her arm in his. "Thanks for worrying about me, but you don't have to."

He frowned at her as if he didn't quite trust her change of attitude. She didn't blame him, but she didn't know how to explain it to him without telling him more than she wanted him to know.

The front door opened and two men, tall and wide, came out. Loud music followed them out into the parking lot. Dean grabbed the door behind them and ushered Sarah inside.

At home, Sarah had rarely hit any bars. A guy she'd dated once had taken her to one for drinks before they went to a play. The place had been dark and subdued, with quiet music and the rustle of whispers.

This was about as far as she could get from that place.

A barrage of sounds and sights assaulted her when they walked into the bar. The chorus of some old rock song pulsed through the air and the level of the conversations going on around them had risen to be heard above the music. Two skinny guys in jeans and leather vests played pool in a corner, with several women in skimpy tops and shorts looking on. A couple other women danced on the small dance floor over by the flashing jukebox.

Dean led her over to the bar. About half of the stools were taken. Sarah climbed up on one of the vacant stools and ran her hands over the smooth surface of the bar. A large mirror reflected the wood-paneled walls and the myriad of motorcycle memorabilia hanging on them.

The bartender, a middle-aged guy with a full head of gray hair, light blue eyes and a ready smile, came over to them.

"What can I get you?"

Dean looked at Sarah and raised a quizzical eyebrow.

"I'll have a beer," she said. She'd never had a beer in her life, but it seemed the thing to drink in a place like this. Beer seemed to go with bars and bikers.

"Got any root beer?" Dean asked.

The bartender shook his head, "Sorry."

"A cola then."

Sarah turned to him when the bartender left to fill their order. "What is it with you and root beer?"

"I like root beer."

There had to be more to it than that. "It's just..."

"Just what?"

"Seems out of character, that's all."

"Oh, yeah?" There was that cocky grin again. "You have a lot of opinions about that. What exactly do you see as my character?"

She shrugged. How did she answer a question like that? She looked him up and down, letting her gaze lazily sweep over him. It was a pretty appealing package, as far as she was concerned, but he did send a certain message.

"Well, take a look at the image you project," she said. "Typical biker. Long hair, pierced ear, motorcycle helmet. Kind of screams booze, you know."

Dean shook his head. "You're stereotyping the biker."

"I am?"

"And you're stereotyping me. You did it earlier today at the park, too. Remember? You said I wasn't the *type* to buy something from that lady."

"But you *are* a biker," she pointed out. "And you *do* have long hair and an earring."

"Look around us. Yeah, you've got your tattoos and long hair, but you've also got those clean-cut guys down at the end of the bar. And some pretty attractive women." He stopped her before she could say more. "Now granted, the bikers who hit a bar like this might be more what you would consider a biker type, but they aren't the only kind of people who ride motorcycles. Doctors, lawyers, teachers, all types of people ride bikes." He smiled as the bartender set their drinks in front of them. "Even those of us who abstain from alcohol."

Sarah took a swig from the beer bottle. Kind of yeasty, but not bad. She took another drink. Cold and wet and pretty darn good. She licked her lips and looked at Dean. She didn't know why she felt compelled to continue the conversation, but she had a feeling there was more to Dean and root beer, if she delved a little deeper. She traced her finger down the side of the bottle. "Have you always abstained?"

Dean laughed, a short, bitter laugh. "I drank my first beer when I was about four or five years old. Didn't take much to get me drunk back then."

Sarah caught her breath. "What?" She clutched her suddenly queasy stomach. "Your parents let you do that?"

He shrugged like it was no big deal. "My old man gave it to me. I guess he thought it was funny to see me drunk." He took a big chug of his cola and set the glass down loudly on the table. "My mom never stood up to him."

Sarah didn't know what to say. She didn't remember Dean's father that well, but she had no idea he would have let his young son get drunk. She stared at the brown bottle. Suddenly the beer didn't taste so good to her.

"I did my share of drinking while I was growing up," Dean went on. His voice sounded very unemotional, carefully so. He took a sip of his soda. "As a teenager, I was all the things everyone accused me of being. But I also saw what alcohol did to my father. I finally realized if I didn't stop, I'd be just like him."

"I never realized..." How could she have lived so close to Dean and his family and have never known? She and Terry had been friends, how could she not have known?

"Well, he usually drank at home. And Terry and I never invited kids over to our house."

"That's right," Sarah said, remembering. "Terry would come over to my house, but I don't think I was ever in yours until a couple days ago."

Dean nodded. "Don't you remember the neighborhood kids laughing at my dad when he'd stagger down the sidewalk?"

"Well, I'd usually try to avoid that group of kids," Sarah said, looking down and dragging her finger through the condensation on the beer bottle. "They laughed at me a lot, too."

Dean reached out and tipped her chin up with one finger. While he gazed into her eyes, he ran that finger across her lips, tracing the frown she hadn't realized had formed there. Her lips tingled where he touched them. "That was a long time ago. Don't let it bother you now."

Sarah knew some of those feelings never went away. Who ever forgot the embarrassment of being teased and laughed at? And might she be the one staggering down the sidewalk before too much longer? Whoa. She didn't want to go there tonight.

She looked around them and noticed the pool table was free. "Hey, Dean. You ever played pool?"

"Yeah, but not for a long time."

"Teach me?"

"You've never played pool?"

She shook her head. "Teach me?" she repeated. She must have gotten a second wind, because now she didn't feel tired at all. Or maybe it was the thought of Dean showing her how to hit those little balls.

Grabbing her beer bottle, she hopped off the stool. She barely limped as she sauntered over to the pool table, confident that Dean would follow her.

When she reached the table, she turned around to see if he did. He was right behind her and so close that she almost stumbled backward. Her hand landed on his chest, to keep herself from falling. He was warm and solid. She was certain she could hear the beating of her heart over the music throbbing through the air.

He reached out and cupped her shoulder to steady her. "Easy," he said.

Yes, it would be so easy to fall for him. Easy to fall for the wild package on the outside, and the softer inside she was discovering as they spent time together.

Sarah snatched her hand away and took a step back. She couldn't fall for him. That would ruin all her plans. All she needed was to end up with a broken heart. This was going to stay strictly physical.

She had to remember that.

She set the beer bottle down on the edge of the pool table and picked up a stick. "Okay, how do I hold this thing?"

"This thing is called a cue stick," Dean told her. He rounded the pool table to stand behind her. He put his arms around her and slowly slid the cue stick along her waist. Then he reached for her left arm and ran his hand gently down the length of it, from shoulder to hand. Shivers followed his hand along her skin. "Lay your arm out like this and rest the cue stick along your thumb. Like this."

He leaned across her back, stretching his arm along hers to position her hand correctly. She had a hard time concentrating on what he was showing her. He was hard and hot pressed against her back, cupped around her butt.

"Wow, I never knew pool could be so enjoyable," she said in a low voice she hoped only he could hear.

He rubbed himself ever so slightly against her and she knew he was enjoying it too. She couldn't resist wiggling her butt a little in response.

Sarah noticed a group of rough-looking men watching them from a table close by. She cleared her throat and stopped wiggling. "So, the object is to hit these little balls with this stick, right?"

"Right." His breath was warm as he spoke softly into her ear. "And get them in these pockets."

She rubbed her cheek lightly against his. Her mouth was so dry she had to swallow before she could speak again. "Pockets. Right."

"Okay, you hold the stick with your other hand, like this." He was wrapped around her so tightly, she was sure they were going to need help to get apart. But all too soon he stepped away with no trouble at all. "Now gently slide the cue across your thumb and try to hit that red ball."

Sarah felt the eyes of the entire bar on her. Her arms were shaking slightly from holding the cue stick so tensely. She glanced at Dean and he smiled at her.

"You can do it," he said. "Just relax."

She nodded and awkwardly jabbed at the ball. It lifted and bounced on the table, knocking into several of the other balls, one of which actually rolled into a pocket. She jumped up and down with joy. She knew that wasn't how it was supposed to be done, but sinking one of those balls into the pocket sent a charge of adrenaline through her. She was ready for more.

He let her practice a few more times and then asked, "So, you ready to play?"

"Ah...sure." She took a long drink of beer. Dean ran over the rules briefly with her and then racked up the balls.

"So, what are we betting?" Dean asked as he rubbed some chalk on the end of his cue stick.

"Betting?" She bet she was going to lose, that's what she bet.

"Sure. Most people bet money, but we could make it more interesting if you like."

The mischievous look on his face made her smile. She sauntered over to him until they were nose to nose. "Oh, really? How interesting?"

He leaned forward until his lips brushed her ear. "How about if I win, I get to be on top tonight?"

Sarah took a deep breath already imagining the weight of his body on hers. "And if I win, you can be on top...in the sleeping bag under the stars."

He shook his head, but she could see the smile he was trying not to let show. "No tent? That could be dangerous."

"No, it would be interesting. You said you wanted interesting."

She couldn't quite decipher his expression, but she swore the smile slipped through. "That I did."

She lost in a matter of minutes. She hoped it wasn't going to rain tonight.

Dean knew they should get going. It would be dark before they found a campground. He hated setting up camp in the dark, stumbling around with a flashlight in one hand and the tent in the other. But he was having too good a time watching Sarah enjoy herself.

He sat at a small table near the bar, chewing the ice cubes in the bottom of his glass and munching on buttered popcorn from a red plastic basket. Sarah had gone up to the bar to buy another round of drinks, but she'd evidently gotten into a conversation with the bartender. He couldn't hear what they were saying, but Sarah was laughing. And so was the bartender.

Something unfamiliar twisted in his gut. If he didn't know better, he'd say it was jealousy. He recognized that glint of lust in the barkeep's eye. Dean knew what the guy wanted when he looked at Sarah that way.

Dean didn't have any business being jealous. Did he?

Two days, he reminded himself. They'd only been on the road two days. But in those two days, she'd managed to get under his skin, tempt him into breaking his promise to himself and then give him some of the best sex of his life. And now she left him hard and aching while he looked forward to more tonight.

Sarah turned back to him with a drink in each hand. Her smile was bright and Dean told himself he imagined the light that turned on in her eyes when she looked at him. She sank into the seat beside him and handed him his Coke.

"That's Ben Pitt," she said, cocking her head toward the bartender. "He's owned this place for ten years. He drives a Harley Road King Classic and his wife left him last year for the Yamaha dealer."

"I thought he looked hungry," Dean muttered.

She frowned. "What?"

"Nothing. How did you find out so much about him in only a couple minutes?"

Sarah shrugged her shoulders. "I asked him if he was Pitt and he said yeah, and rest kind of tumbled out of his mouth. I think he liked talking to someone new."

Dean laughed. "I think he liked talking to you."

"Well, yeah, because I haven't heard it all before."

Dean glanced up at Ben Pitt, who still had his eye on Sarah. He caught Dean's stare and quickly moved down to the other end of the bar. "More likely because you're a pretty young woman and he wanted you to know he drives a nice bike and was a lonely guy."

"Oh, no, I don't think so." But Sarah glanced curiously over her shoulder. A slow smile spread across her face. "You really think so?"

"Trust me." As soon as the words were out of his mouth, he wanted to take them back. Wrong choice of words.

She put her hand on his. "I do."

Oh, great. All he'd been doing was lying to her. Would she forgive him if he told her the truth, or would she be furious with him? He didn't want to find out.

He told himself it didn't matter. In a few days they would be parting ways and they'd never see each other again. She could keep her fantasy and he would never have to admit to her that he had lied.

But why did the thought of never seeing her again leave him feeling empty inside?

A slow song played from the jukebox. Sarah set down her beer bottle. "Dance with me?"

Wrap his arms around her soft curves? Rub hips together to the music? Showing her how to shoot pool had almost killed him. He ached so bad he couldn't take much more. He shook his head and the wistful smile on her face faded away. "I'm not much of a dancer." He pushed his glass away. "Let's go find a campground."

"Well, I want to dance." She looked around the room. Dean could tell the moment she set her eye on a young guy with blond hair and leathers sitting by himself across the room. "Excuse me."

Damned if she didn't walk right over to him bold as can be and ask him to dance with her.

The sly grin on the biker's face nearly brought Dean out of his chair. He clenched his fists beneath the table and watched the guy follow Sarah onto the dance floor and put his arms around her.

She didn't seem to mind. She put her arms around him too and swayed with him to the music. Her laughter floated low and sexy across the room. Dean looked away before he did something he might regret.

So that's the way she wanted to play it. Dean leaned back in his chair and swept his gaze around the room. He saw a couple cute young things on the other side of the pool table. They were blonde and leggy, with skimpy tops and wet, red lips. They were eyeing him as if he were a piece of candy. It was obvious they wouldn't mind if he came over and sat down beside them.

He almost rose and crossed the floor. He almost introduced himself and bought them drinks. A week ago he would have. He'd have turned on the charm and flirted with them and thought nothing of it.

But tonight he thought of nothing but Sarah.

He swung his gaze back around to the dance floor. The guy was holding Sarah much closer than he had been a minute ago. Sarah was still smiling, but she wasn't laughing any more. The jerk's hands were roaming all over her back.

Dean sat up in his chair. He watched the hands creep lower down Sarah's body. When his hands stretched out to cup her ass, a growl started deep in Dean's throat. He sprang to his feet and covered the distance to the dance floor in only a few long strides.

He tapped the guy on the shoulder. "Excuse me, I'm cutting in."

The guy snarled at Dean and swung Sarah away from him. "Find your own girl."

Dean grabbed his shoulder and pulled him away from her. "This *is* my girl."

Sarah stumbled backward when the jerk let go of her. Dean grasped her arms to steady her. She smiled up at Dean before she turned to look at the guy slinking his way back to his table.

"Bye, Stu," she said lightly. "Thanks for the dance." She turned back into Dean's embrace. She rested her head on his chest and rubbed her face against his shirt.

"Hi," she said softly. He could hear the smile in her voice.

"Hi, yourself." He swayed to the music, soaking in the feel of Sarah against him. The warmth of her body seemed to seep into his bones, heating him more thoroughly than the sun ever did.

"I hoped you'd come." She curled her arms around his back. "He doesn't dance as well as you do."

"Oh, and how would you know how well I dance?"

"I just knew," she murmured into his shirt.

When the slow song wound down and a new song started rocking and rolling, she started to pull away from him. Dean held onto her tightly even though it was sweet torture. He'd just gotten her into his arms; he sure wasn't going to let her go.

"Dean?"

"Shhh. I like this song." He didn't even know what song it was. All he cared about was holding Sarah.

"But it's a fast song."

He gathered her closer. "I don't care. Who says you can't slow dance to a fast song?"

She snuggled against him. "Not me."

He couldn't resist planting a light kiss on the top of her head. He didn't want to try to decipher the feelings stirring up in him as he held Sarah. He didn't want to think too hard about it.

But he smiled at the thought of rescuing her from that heavy-handed loser.

Get real, Bastian.

These feelings bubbling up in him had nothing to do with being protective. He didn't rescue Sarah as much as claim her.

Claim her?

Sarah's hands began tracing slow circles along his back. He melted into her, her hands working magic on him. Two days, and already he couldn't imagine a day without her touch. A day without her smile.

What was he thinking? He'd never met a woman he couldn't walk away from.

Or had he finally done exactly that?

The thought made him stop and take a step back, looking down at the woman in his arms. She gazed sleepily up at him, her hair slightly mussed, her lips partly open. He could imagine waking up to her looking like this for the rest of his life.

The thought didn't scare him as much as he imagined it would.

"Hey," he murmured. "Think it's about time to find a place for the night?"

She nodded and grinned. "Remember, I get to be on the bottom."

Chapter Seven

"This is fun," Sarah said with a laugh.

Fun?

Dean looked up at her from where he knelt on the hard ground. He found himself smiling back in spite of himself. She held the flashlight for him while he tried to set up the tent. Yards of blue nylon spread out before him, refusing to cooperate. He may not have been happy about doing this in the dark, but the sound of Sarah's laughter made it all worthwhile.

"Keep the light still," he growled. But even he could hear the amusement in his voice.

"I'm doing my best. You're being awfully slow."

The light shot off to the trees and Dean glanced over to see her looking up at the sky.

"Where are the stars tonight?" she asked. He couldn't see the pout, but he could hear it in her voice.

"Hiding with the moon behind all those storm clouds," Dean replied dryly. "Can I have some light please?"

"Sorry." She brought the flashlight beam back down where it belonged.

"Oh well, I guess I couldn't have slept under the stars tonight anyway."

"Don't sound so disappointed," Dean said. "You'll have other chances."

"What do we have, only a couple more nights on the road?" she asked.

"Two or three, depending on how many more town fairs you drag me to."

He lost the light again. This time she'd dropped her arm and the light shone down onto the grass. "You had a good time too. I know you did."

Yes, he had, but only because he'd been with her. He wasn't able to say the words out loud, though. What good would it do to admit it to her?

"Time is flying already," she said. "We'll be in Denver soon and the trip will be all over."

"We have a lot of miles yet to go," Dean told her.

"Good," she said softly.

He understood how she felt, and it was a little unnerving. He was reluctant to see the trip end too. He didn't want to think too much yet about the reason. The idea that he actually wanted to stick around with Sarah was going to take some getting used to.

He stood up. That was the longest it had ever taken to set up that little tent. Must have been because of the blonde he had on his mind.

"Thank you for today," she said.

"It was nothing." He turned away to stack some wood in the fire pit.

"Yes it was. You stopped at a little town fair for me. You took me to a biker bar. You rescued me from the octopus on the dance floor."

"That was my pleasure."

She sighed. "Still my hero."

"Hero? What are you taking about?"

"You've always been my hero, didn't you know that?"

He looked up from the pile of kindling he was lighting. "I was the guy who was a bad influence on all the other kids, remember?"

"Yeah, I remember," she said, lifting an eyebrow. "I remember Kyle Jones and Jimmy Clark backing me into a corner. I remember crying so hard I could barely see through the tears in my eyes. They'd knocked the books out of my hands and were stealing the food from my lunch box. And suddenly Kyle went flying through the air. And Jimmy ran home with a bloody nose." Sarah sat down on the log beside where Dean knelt. "You picked up my books and my lunch. You wiped my tears with the edge of your shirt."

Dean shifted uneasily. When did the ground get so hard? "I didn't do any more than anyone else would do."

"Those bullies had been picking on me for weeks," she said. "I lived in constant terror of them. No one else did anything. But you rescued me. And after that they never bothered me again."

Yeah, he'd searched those two out and let them know what would happen to them if they ever messed with Sarah again.

He'd always remembered how she looked up at him that morning, after those two animals ran off with their tails between their legs. Her eyes were filled with tears, her cute little nose red and runny. And she gave him a smile that lit up his whole world.

He'd never forgotten that smile.

Dean sat back on the grass to give his knees a rest. He stared into the growing flames. Some of the kids he worked with had favored him with some pretty awesome smiles over the years, but none of them compared with Sarah's that day.

That smile had gotten him through some pretty rough times over the next few years. When his father tore him down and told him how rotten he was, Dean would conjure up that smile in his mind and he could turn off the drunken ravings. When people in the neighborhood told him he was no good, he'd remember that smile and walk away.

Dean turned to look at Sarah and found her beaming back at him.

He had her in his arms before he even knew he was reaching for her. She landed on his lap, straddling his waist with her thighs. Her breasts flattened against his chest as he squeezed her tight.

He was certain he meant only to give her a hug to thank her for helping him stick it out long enough to get his high school diploma. For letting him know that she believed there was a good person behind the tough façade he'd built up over the years. For helping him make a new life for himself, because with that simple smile she had let him know there was a lot more to him than his father said there was.

She was *his* hero.

But somehow, the easy embrace gradually changed into something else. Something more. Sarah wiggled atop his thighs, snuggling even closer to him. He slid his hands beneath her shirt, to caress the soft skin on her back. She nibbled on his neck, leaving a trail of wet kisses from his shoulder to his ear.

He gasped when he felt her tongue begin to play with the diamond in his ear.

He never knew shivers could run through his whole body, but they did when Sarah's tongue tangled with his earring. Quivers of desire started there, ran down his neck and spread out in all directions. His blood coursed faster through his veins, tracing the paths of desire.

He cupped her face and captured her mouth, sweeping his tongue along her slick lips. Sarah moaned and plunged her tongue into his mouth. He sucked lightly on it, drinking in her sweetness. He grew hard beneath her tight little bottom.

Maybe he'd let her be on top after all.

Sarah laughed lightly into his mouth. Curious enough to break the kiss, Dean leaned back to look at her. Her back was to the fire, so her face was in the shadows, and he couldn't read her expression.

"What?"

"I just thought of something." She paused and cleared her throat. "Never mind. I probably shouldn't say anything."

"Then let's get back to kissing." He kissed the top of her nose.

She laughed again.

"What?"

"I can't believe it. This is my fantasy come true."

"What?" He knew he sounded like a parrot but he didn't have a clue what she was talking about.

She put her hands up to her cheeks. "I'm blushing."

"I can't tell," Dean said, impatient to get back to that incredible mouth. "It's too dark."

"I...I had a major crush on you when I was a teenager," she said. "I bet you never knew that."

He sat back a little. "No, I didn't."

"Well, you were already my hero. When I got old enough to have a crush, who else would I have it on?"

"I wish I'd known. I would have paid more attention to you."

"No, you wouldn't. You would have been as embarrassed as

I'd have been, if you'd ever found out about it. You would have avoided me like a radar trap. I was only thirteen when you were seventeen. I was just one of the little kids in the neighborhood. Back then, four years was a big difference."

She was right. If he knew one of Terry's friends had a crush on him, even if it was Sarah, he would have been embarrassed and horrified. He would have kept even more distance than he already had.

"Now that I'm confessing," she said with a light laugh, "I might as well admit that this is exactly like one of the daydreams I had about you."

Daydreams? Sarah used to have fantasies about him? It took him a minute to wrap his mind around that idea. "It is?"

"Yeah. You spirited me away to a dark and secret place on your motorcycle. We drove through the neighborhood first, so everyone could see that I was with you, the bad boy. The rebel. I felt special because you singled me out. I felt special because I was rebelling a little too. And you know I never did that."

"No, you didn't," Dean said slowly. He had a feeling he knew where this was going, and suddenly, he knew he didn't want to hear it.

"You took me to a quiet, secluded place like this. And I sat in your lap exactly like this. And you kissed me like I was the sweetest thing on earth." Sarah's words came out on a sigh as she remembered her daydream. "There I was, kissing the boy I wasn't supposed to have anything to do with. It was so daring. So exciting. Love 'em and Leave 'em Bastian was loving me!"

She doesn't want to do it with you, a voice deep inside him said. She wants to do it with the bad boy. She wants to do it with the rebel.

He should have never given into temptation last night. How could he have made love to her when he'd done nothing but lie to her from the beginning? No wonder she only wanted a quick fling. She thought he was still the same guy she had a crush on. Why wouldn't she? He'd led her to believe that's exactly who he was.

He couldn't make love to her again pretending to be someone else.

Sarah wiggled on his lap again. "Let's get back to kissing before I embarrass myself even more."

Although it was one of the hardest things he'd ever done, Dean put his hands on her waist and lifted her off his lap. He understood the confusion he saw when she faced the firelight, but he couldn't come up with any words to comfort her.

She continued to stare into the fire when she said, "What did I say? What did I do?"

"Nothing," he said gruffly. "It's getting late. You take the tent again. I'll sleep outside."

"You don't want to sleep in there with me?"

He didn't answer, but stood up and walked away before he gathered her back into his arms.

"But what about the bet?"

He grabbed the sleeping bag roll off the bike and tossed it down on the opposite side of the fire. He didn't turn around until he heard her go into the tent.

What the hell happened? Sarah sat in the middle of the tent and yanked her jeans off. What a jerk. She blinked away the tears that sprang to her eyes. He'd blown his chance, dammit. She wasn't throwing herself at him ever again. She'd had enough rejection to last a lifetime.

She pulled off her T-shirt and pitched it against the wall of the tent. What happened out there?

Last night had been wonderful. At least for her. Exciting. Passionate. Emotional. Maybe it hadn't been for him. Maybe he didn't want more.

But then why the bet? Why did he hold her hand in the park? Why did he press against her playing pool? Slow dance with her? Pull her into his arms tonight?

What made him change his mind?

She plopped down onto the sleeping bag and punched the towel she used as a pillow. Was it something she said? Was it finding out she had a crush on him years ago? Why would that matter? She punched the pillow again. She was done trying to figure him out

What a jerk!

She woke up when thunder rumbled through the air and echoed around her. She could see flashes of lightning through the walls of the tent. She got up on her knees and unzipped the flap.

In the fading glow of the campfire, she could almost make out a dark mound on the other side of the campsite. It hadn't started raining yet, but it surely would soon.

"Dean," she called in a loud whisper. "Dean, wake up."

No answer.

She called again a little louder, but he still didn't respond. The heck with him. If the jerk wanted to sleep through a thunderstorm, let him.

But a few minutes later, the rain came in a downpour, almost as if a pail of water had been dumped from the sky. She turned on the flashlight and looked out from the tent but couldn't see anything through the sheets of rain.

"Dean!" she called, louder this time. "Get in here!"

She thought she heard footsteps over the thundering rain, but she wasn't sure. Then suddenly he appeared in the beam of the flashlight, soaked to the skin, wearing only drenched boxer shorts. Sarah reached for the towel she'd used as a pillow while he crawled inside, bringing all that water with him.

"Here," she said, tossing him the towel.

Dean crouched inside the doorway. Water dripped off his long hair and ran down his muscled arms. Sarah couldn't drag her eyes away as she watched him run the towel across his broad chest and down his taut abdomen. She ran her tongue over her lips as she imagined herself licking those beads of water off his magnificent body.

Dean looked down at the puddle of water growing by his knees. "Sorry."

Sarah raised an eyebrow.

"I know," he said. "I'm sorry about last night. I should have come in the tent with you to begin with."

"I didn't say it," Sarah replied, "but I'm glad you did."

He slowly stopped drying off with the towel as he stared at her. His eyes looked even darker in the shadows. "Now I'm even more sorry I didn't come in here sooner."

Sarah looked down and realized she wore only a bra and panties, some of the lacy ones she'd bought at Victoria's Secret on the off-chance Dean might catch a glimpse of her changing. She was glad now that she took the time.

She cleared her throat. "Um, you should get out of those."

"My boxers?"

"Yeah. They're soaked."

She switched off the flashlight. The sound of wet cloth squeaking against wet skin made her heart pound faster. So did the loud splat. In an instant, Dean was beside her on the sleeping bag. And the tent seemed much smaller than it had a few moments ago.

Rain battered the tent, causing more noise than she would have thought possible. Thunder rumbled around them. And still, Sarah swore she could hear the pounding of her heart. Or was it Dean's?

Not being able to see Dean but knowing that he lay naked beside her made her blood surge through her veins. Then, as if it had a mind of its own, her hand reached out to touch him. Her fingers brushed his shoulder and she discovered that he was lying on his side, facing her.

"Beautiful Sarah," he whispered.

He touched her shoulder. His fingers glided down her arm, sending waves of awareness rushing along her skin. He drew his fingers back up her arm, stopping at the thin bra strap. She caught her breath when he slid his finger beneath the strap and drew it down over her shoulder. Then he leaned forward and kissed the top of the shoulder where the strap had rested.

Last night's lovemaking had been fast and frantic. Tonight, now that they were sheltered from the storm, the pace was slower, sweeter. Her heart swelled as she realized she'd been given another chance to experience passion with Dean.

She stroked his strong back with her hands and drew him closer, all the while reveling in the tingles his lips left on her skin. As his kisses rained across her chest, his hand dropped down her back to the bra clasp. He expertly released it with one hand.

"You're very good at that," Sarah said, for some reason feeling a little irritated.

He chuckled lightly. "Thank you."

"You must have had a lot of practice."

"Not as much as you think."

"Yeah, but..."

"Shhh," he said, and silenced her as his lips covered hers.

His mouth should be illegal, the tantalizing things he made her feel. All the electrical charges up in the stormy sky couldn't match the sparks of passion shooting through her body right now. Her senses were on fire, reacting to Dean's slightest touch.

She touched him in return, loving the sensation of his hard muscles and smooth skin beneath her hand. She skimmed her fingers along his side and she felt him shiver.

"Are you cold?" she asked, pulling her mouth away only far enough to form the words. Her lips brushed against his as she spoke. "We can get inside the sleeping bag."

"How could I be cold with your arms around me?"

"You always know the right thing to say, don't you?"

"Not always."

She knew he must have had loads of well-rehearsed lines, but she wouldn't let that bother her tonight. She'd never heard them before and right now she'd let herself believe he meant them just for her.

Dean drew her bra straps down her arms and tossed it away. Then he used his mouth for something much more pleasing than mere words. He took one of her swollen nipples between his lips and tugged gently, sucking it into his mouth.

Desire shot deep to her very core. Dampness gathered between her legs and the tension there began to grow. The staccato of rain on the tent seemed to echo the urgency building within her. The need was growing too fast. She wanted to savor the sensations. Memorize each detail.

She dropped her head back and let herself experience, just for a moment, Dean making love to her breast. He cupped its fullness in his hands, laved the sensitive skin with his tongue. Raked the nipple gently with his teeth.

She couldn't bear much more. And yet they had just begun.

She combed her fingers through his wet hair, pulling him closer to her. He smelled like the rain. She licked the beads of water from his shoulder.

He lifted his head from her breast and put his arms around her, gathering her body to his. His hard thighs tangled with her legs. His chest became a pillow for her swollen breasts. And her hips pressed intimately against the evidence of his desire.

"I'm sorry I pushed you away," he whispered in her ear.

She sighed. "Why did you?"

"I can't remember why," he said, brushing his lips against hers. "It doesn't matter anymore." He drew her even closer, crushing her breasts against him, pushing his hardness against her soft belly.

She rocked back and forth against him, rubbing herself against his hard thigh. It felt so good, but she needed more. Much more. The frenzy within her built rapidly. To heck with savoring the moment. "Please, Dean..."

"Not so fast," he said lightly. He cupped her breasts in his hands and sprinkled kisses over her heated skin. "I want you to enjoy this too."

"Oh, I'm enjoying this," she gasped. "I really, really am."

Dean chuckled softly. He took one of her nipples into his hot mouth, drawing it far inside. His wet hair tickled her breasts, cooling her sensitive skin. But when he sucked deeply, she was hot again. Needy again. Aching.

"Dean, please!" she cried.

He caught the edge of her panties with his fingers and slid his hand underneath. She lifted her hips and he stripped them from her body. He reached down between their bodies and found the damp center of her desire. When his fingers danced on her sensitive bud, her body jerked in response.

Was that thunder crashing around them, or was her blood pounding in her ears? Was that lightning flashing before her eyes or the fireworks her body experienced as Dean's fingers played with her body?

"Oh, Dean," she breathed, and then she could speak no more. She gasped and gave herself over to the sensations he caused in her. Sparks of pleasure rained over her, more and more, coming faster and faster. Finally, and all too soon, she burst into a million flashes of lightning. Her body convulsed around him as she rocked with the release she'd been craving.

When she could finally move again, when she could breathe again without gasping, she drew him into her arms. "Come here," she said, opening her legs for him. "You get to be on top."

She felt Dean rise above her and she held her breath in anticipation. But instead of sliding into her waiting body, he cursed and flopped down onto the floor of the tent. "I can't."

She reached out to him, touched his thigh, tried not to feel rejected again. "What is it? Why not?"

"The condoms are out in the saddle bag."

"Oh." She definitely didn't feel rejected. She rose up on her knees and found his erection. She stroked the soft, hard flesh and smiled when she heard him groan with pleasure. Then she bent over and took his velvet shaft into her mouth. Just once. Just enough to get him wet and wanting even more.

"Hold that thought," she said.

Then the new Sarah rose up and did something the old Sarah would have never considered. She dashed out of the tent into the pouring rain, stark naked. The blast of water nearly took her breath away. She ran as fast as she could to the

115

motorcycle and grabbed the saddlebag.

Drenched, she brought it into the tent and handed it to Dean. He switched on the flashlight and beamed it on her first. She grabbed the towel he had used earlier and began to towel off the best she could.

And Dean watched.

Desire began to build in her again when she knew Dean's eyes were on her. She slowed her strokes with the towel, imagining Dean's hands on her instead. She swept the towel over her breasts, lifting them up and pressing them together as she slowly dried her skin. She took her time with each leg, leisurely caressing the length of each. Her stomach was next, and then she lowered her hand. When she started to lazily rub the towel between her legs, Dean cursed.

"Enough," he said, the word almost a strangled sound coming from his throat. He focused the flashlight into his saddlebag and rummaged through it, tossing half the contents onto the floor.

Sarah wiped off her feet and dropped the towel when she was done. Dean finally pulled out a little gold package from his saddlebag before he switched off the flashlight.

She joined him on the sleeping bag. "I liked being able to see you. Can't we leave the flashlight on?"

He swept his fingers along her shoulder and down to her breast. "Yeah, if you want to put on a show for any of the other campers who might look out of their tents. Our silhouettes would be right there for anyone to see."

"Oh." Had anyone been looking when she did her little show with the towel for Dean? She didn't want to know, but oddly enough, the possibility didn't bother her as much as she thought it would. She never knew she had an exhibitionist streak.

"Never mind. I don't need to see you. I can feel you." She swept her hand over him, starting with the top of his wet head, along his neck and shoulder, then down his arm until she found the condom package in his hand. "Let me."

She took the package from him and opened it, fumbling with it a little in the dark. When she was ready, she took her time smoothing the protection over him, rubbing him from tip to base in long, slow strokes.

Dean groaned. "Do you know what you're doing to me?"

She stroked him one more time. "I sure hope so."

He grabbed her shoulders and drew her down on top of him. In a smooth motion, he rolled over, poised on top of her.

She knew he'd waited long enough. She understood the urgency. She was ready for him and opened herself to him. He entered her swiftly, filling her completely. She wrapped her legs around him and pulled him even closer to her, if that was possible. Even in the darkness, she kept her eyes open. Although she couldn't see him, she could imagine his eyes staring into hers as he rode her through the storm.

As he plunged into her, filling her over and over, tension began to build inside her again. Her breath hitched as those intense sensations buzzed along her skin, shot through her body, and concentrated at that spot between her legs. She rocked her hips against him, trying to find the friction she needed.

Dean ran his hand along her side and slipped his fingers between their bodies. When he touched her clit, the pressure was all she needed to explode again with a burst of sensations.

He cried out with his release a moment later. She held him close, murmuring his name as they came down together. He kissed her neck and sighed, his breath warm against her skin. "Wow."

"Wow," she agreed.

A few minutes later, he slipped out of her and said, "I'll be right back."

After he'd taken care of the condom, he lay back down beside her and brought her close to him again. She laid her head on his shoulder and snuggled against him. She knew she could spend the rest of her life lying in Dean's arms.

And just when she thought this might be the most perfect night of her life, her legs began to twitch uncontrollably.

"Are you okay?" Dean asked, rolling slightly away from her.

She tried to joke even as she wanted to cry. "Yeah, you...tired me out. It's been a long time since my legs had such a workout two nights in a row."

He chuckled and rubbed her legs like he had after that first night on the road. As quickly as it had started, the twitching stopped. He took her back into his arms and quickly fell asleep.

Sarah laid awake for a long time afterward, tension tightening her stomach. She never knew what was going to happen to her body next. Never knew which symptom would rear its ugly head when she least expected it. Was this the way she would spend the rest of her life, anxiously waiting for the next surprise attack?

Was this as good as she was ever going to be?

Chapter Eight

Sarah woke up to the sound of voices outside the tent. When she opened her eyes, the sun shone through the lightweight walls, bathing them in a pale blue glow. She found herself wrapped around Dean's bare back, her arms across his chest, her legs tangled with his.

Sometime during the night the rain had stopped.

She reluctantly eased herself away, even though her body begged to stay close to Dean. She sat up and simply watched him sleep for a moment. Her chest filled with an emotion she was afraid to name.

With the lightest of touches, she brushed the dark hair away from his face. She gazed at the strong jaw, the shadow of a beard. He had a slight smile on his face. He looked happy. Content. Dare she say, satisfied?

And, looking at him, she had to admit that he made her satisfied. Content.

He made her happy.

Oh, no. She clamped her hand over her mouth before the cry could escape. How had this happened?

Not the lovemaking. She knew perfectly well how that had happened. And it had been wonderful. Everything she'd dreamed of and more. But this situation hadn't ended up the way she'd planned. She'd been naïve enough to believe if she had one or two memorable nights of sex with Dean, she could go back to Buffalo a happy woman.

But now, the memories weren't enough. A few nights weren't enough.

She wanted more. She wanted Dean. She wanted happily ever after.

Sarah angrily brushed away the tears that slipped from her eyes. What was wrong with her? She knew better. She knew what she couldn't have. But it obviously didn't matter.

She had fallen in love with Dean.

Stupid. How could she be so stupid? Falling in love with him was the last thing she wanted to do. She thought she knew what she had been getting into. She thought she had her emotions under control.

Now she looked down at the man sleeping beside her and knew she would go back to Buffalo with a broken heart.

The voices outside got a little louder. She scrambled into a damp T-shirt and shorts. Pushing aside the wet towel and boxers that still lay crumpled on the floor just inside the door, she unzipped the tent and peeked outside.

Two teenaged boys were standing by Dean's motorcycle, gazing at it in something close to awe. Sarah turned to rouse Dean and discovered that he was already awake. He gazed at her with an intensity that sent shivers along her skin.

"Good morning," he said, his voice sleep-rough and way too inviting.

She dropped the tent flap. No one should look that fabulous first thing in the morning. She couldn't help but smile. And hope he didn't notice the tears.

"Hi," she replied, pleased that her voice sounded light. She cocked her head in the direction of the Harley. "You have some fans outside."

He didn't appear to be in any hurry to move, or to get any clothes on for that matter. Her body heated as he ran his gaze over her.

He reached out to her. "Come here."

It would only make things worse to feel his arms around her this morning. She didn't need a reminder of what she would be leaving behind. She shook her head. "You have a couple kids out there drooling all over your bike."

"I'll wash it." He dropped his arms down to his side but didn't move. His gaze continued to warm her and she couldn't stop looking at his long, beautiful legs. His broad, muscular chest. And the obvious evidence of his desire for her.

"I want to touch you again," he said, his smooth voice and bright eyes a seductive combination. "I want to feel your hands on me too."

She closed her eyes and turned her head away. Her body remembered too easily how it felt to be pressed against his. How his skin felt beneath her fingers. "Dean..."

"What's the matter?"

"Nothing," she lied. As soon as she was certain no tears were going to trickle down her cheeks, she looked at him again. "I don't feel comfortable fooling around in here with those kids only a few feet away."

"All right. I'll go along with that." He grabbed his saddlebag and pulled out some dry clothing. Then he looked up at her and winked. "Think about me today. We might just have to turn in early tonight."

How could she tell him she didn't dare risk making love with him again? Her heart couldn't take it. She knelt down and dug into her saddlebag to find her cell phone.

"I'm gonna call my mom," she said. "I promised her I would and I haven't yet. She's probably imagining the worst."

She followed Dean out of the tent. The grass was soggy beneath her feet. He stepped over a puddle and joined the guys standing beside his Harley. He started talking easily with them. Soon they were laughing together. The light-hearted sound should have made her smile. Instead, she wanted to cry.

He was in love with her.

Dean wasn't sure his mind had wrapped itself around the concept yet, but his heart seemed to have opened up and embraced the news. Was he crazy? Or was it about time?

The two bike fans had finally walked away and Dean watched Sarah as she talked to her mother. His heart swelled with overflowing emotions he never expected to feel. She paced around the campsite, her gait a little uneven on the soggy ground.

He must have tired her out last night. The thought made him grin.

The phone was up to her ear and her cute little legs stretched out from the loose shorts. He remembered how they'd felt wrapped around him and he hardened again.

He started packing up the tent, trying to get used to the idea of feeling what he had been sure he never would. When had it happened? When had he fallen?

The first night, when they came together in a burst of passion? Last night, when they danced together in the bar? Or even earlier, like when she smiled up at him with her lunch box at her feet and tears streaming down her face?

She was everything he'd ever wanted. Pretty, funny,

sensual, adventurous. He could easily imagine spending the rest of his life with her. Could he overcome his rough childhood with Sarah by his side?

Could he even imagine raising a family with Sarah?

That thought was a little too frightening, but maybe he could get used to the idea. Dean attached the first saddlebag to the Harley. Suddenly, thinking about having Sarah in his life, anything seemed possible.

She might have told him she only wanted them to be together for this trip, but he knew she didn't really mean it. She only said it because she thought he was still the bad boy.

He'd lied to her from day one. His grin slipped from his face. He glanced over his shoulder to Sarah as she laughed into the cell phone. He grabbed the second saddlebag. What would she say when she found out he wasn't on the road with Aerosmith as he'd let her believe?

Wouldn't she forgive him if he confessed that he'd fallen in love with her? Wouldn't she be happy to find out he was actually considering marriage? Marriage? Dean dropped the saddlebag on his foot. And...and children. Impossible thoughts for him such a short time ago.

Wouldn't she forgive him once she found out the truth?

Maybe. If she wasn't furious at him for lying to her to begin with. He picked the saddlebag back up and attached it to the bike.

He'd have to confess to her tonight. His stomach actually turned a little at the thought. But he told himself she'd forgive him once she realized he was no longer Love 'em and Leave 'em Bastian. She'd be so happy with the truth that she'd forgive the lies.

They'd spend the night warming up the tent with the passion that simmered between them. Yeah, he could picture

123

that already.

She walked over to him and tucked her cell phone into her saddlebag. "Mom says hello."

She didn't look him in the eye. Not a good sign. "How is your mom?"

"Fine."

Was she nervous because he'd been a jerk last night? Was she afraid he was going to pull away from her again? Well, he could ease her mind on that. He closed the space between them and gathered her into his arms. She stiffened for a moment and he thought she was going to be the one to pull away.

What was the matter? Was she afraid she couldn't trust him? He was afraid to ask her, because right now he couldn't be sure what her answer would be.

But a moment later she relaxed and put her arms around him as well.

"Good morning," she whispered in his ear.

"Yes, it is," he replied. There was no better way to start a morning than with Sarah in his arms.

"I think we better stick to the interstate today," he told her and kissed her neck lightly. "We'll get some good miles in and stop at a campground early enough that we can dry all those wet things I stuffed in the plastic bag."

She nodded and stepped away from him. He couldn't decipher the expression on her face.

"Okay."

He frowned. "Are you all right?"

She seemed to shake herself out of whatever mood she was in. She beamed him a smile and he could almost believe it was real. "Absolutely," she said brightly. "Let's get this show on the road."

Dean smiled back. His Harley and the woman he loved. It didn't get any better than this.

The road had taken its toll on Sarah.

The sun was hot, the air humid, the miles long. She could barely drag herself off the bike when they reached the campground in Missouri. She purposely dropped to a sitting position on the ground before her legs could give out on her and send her sprawling.

It was the heat. It must have been the heat. Sarah vaguely remembered the neurologist warning her against getting overheated. He said so many things that day, they were all jumbled in a brain that felt, at the moment, as if it was packed with cotton.

"Are you okay?" Dean asked.

"Yeah, just give me a minute," she replied. Her limbs felt like lead weights. She wanted to curl up into a ball and go to sleep. But that would be a sure sign to Dean that something definitely wasn't okay. If she could only make it a couple more days.

"No problem," Dean said, dropping cross-legged on the ground beside her. "I keep forgetting you're not used to this many hours on the bike. Sorry."

"Don't apologize. I invited myself on this trip, remember?"

"Oh, yeah." He hopped up easily and grabbed the tent off the bike. "You rest. I'll set up camp."

She watched him pitch the tent and start the fire. When he pulled the plastic bag full of wet laundry from where it had been stuffed in his saddlebag, Sarah knew she had to get up and get going. She struggled to her feet. As she started toward him, she nearly tripped on the slightly uneven ground. Her foot was dragging again and she couldn't seem to do anything about it.

All she could do was hope Dean wouldn't notice. Luckily, their campsite wasn't far from the camp office building that housed a good-sized laundry room.

"I can take care of that," she said. With any luck, the laundry room would have air conditioning and she would be able to cool off.

"Thanks," Dean replied.

"If you have any other dirty clothes, you can put them with this stuff. Might as well get a full load."

He pulled a few things out of his saddlebag and added them to the clothes in the plastic bag. "While you're doing that, I'm going to see what they've got in the store."

"Okay." Sarah was relieved when he turned away from her and headed for the camp store. That way he couldn't see her struggle to walk with her arms full of dirty, wet clothing and her foot dragging on the ground. Tears filled her eyes. At the rate she was going, she'd need a cane before too much longer.

There were chairs in a corner of the laundry room and a table with some out-of-date magazines. And blissful air conditioning. Sarah sank gratefully into a chair once the washer started and grabbed an old *Better Homes and Gardens* magazine.

She'd flipped through almost the entire magazine when a short, middle-aged woman dressed in colorful shorts and top came in with a laundry basket piled nearly to overflowing.

She saw Sarah sitting in the corner and smiled. "Hi, there. You using all these machines?"

Sarah dropped the magazine down onto the table. "Ah, no. Just one."

The woman started stuffing laundry into several of the

washing machines. "Only one? Haven't been on the road long, huh? Or are you traveling alone?"

"No, there's two of us."

"Well, there's two of us too, but we seem to go through a lot of clothes. Especially when it's so hot. Everything gets sweaty, you know?"

Sarah nodded. The woman looked like she knew what she was doing. She brought her own detergent and softener, and she had a container filled with quarters.

"Have you been traveling long?" Sarah asked.

"Oh, honey, that's all we do," the woman said with a laugh. "John and I have been full-timing for three years now."

"Full-timing?"

"My husband and I took early retirement. Sold our house and bought a motor home. We've been traveling the country, seeing the sights, meeting new people." She held out her hand. "Marge Berrey, pleased to meet you."

Sarah shook Marge's hand and introduced herself. "Wow, what a life, huh?"

Marge sat down beside her. "It's the best."

The possibilities whirled through Sarah's mind. "I'll bet every day's an adventure."

"When we want it to be," Marge said. She pulled some yellow yarn and a crochet hook out of a small canvas bag. Almost instantly her fingers sent the crochet hook flying. "Other times, like now, we stay in one place for a while. Put our feet up. Get the laundry caught up. Then we're ready to take off again."

"What are you making?" Sarah asked.

"We have a new grandchild due to be born next month. This is a blanket for the little one. My daughter and her

127

husband live in Texas. That's where we'll head when we leave here."

Time flew by while Sarah chatted with Marge, hearing stories of their travels, of visiting Mt. Rushmore, the Grand Canyon and family all over the country. This must be what Dean's life was like, traveling with the band. Seeing new places, meeting new people, never knowing from one day to another exactly what was going to happen.

By the time the laundry was finished, Sarah longed for more than happily ever after with Dean.

She wanted a life of adventure *and* happily ever after with Dean.

Life liked to play games with people, with their hopes and dreams. Why did she long for the kind of life that she could never have?

Sarah took a deep breath and pushed those thoughts out of her mind. What was the point of dwelling on it? Was it better to have never known the things you couldn't have, or to experience for a short while what you couldn't keep?

When Dean stepped into the room, Sarah's heart swelled with the love she felt for him. She couldn't regret going on this trip with him. She couldn't regret falling in love with him. What was that old saying about it being better to have loved and lost...?

She introduced him to Marge and hoped the butterflies that flew into her stomach at the sight of him didn't make her voice flutter as well. But no one looked at her strangely so she must have sounded pretty normal. She doubted she'd ever feel normal again. Dean helped her fold the laundry and they said good-bye to Marge.

Sarah realized she felt a lot better after sitting in the air-conditioned room. Must be the heat made her symptoms worse.

Her mind felt pretty clear now and she wasn't even walking too badly. Maybe she wasn't ready for that cane yet after all.

When they got back to the campsite, Sarah saw that Dean had their dinner ready. Or at least the makings of dinner. Hot dogs, buns, condiments and long, pointed sticks lay across the picnic table. And, of course, root beer.

"You probably won't believe me if I tell you I've never done this before," Sarah said when Dean speared a hot dog on a stick and handed it to her.

He looked up at her. "Never? Weren't you ever a Girl Scout?"

She shook her head. "Nope."

He gestured toward the fire. "It's pretty self-explanatory. If you have any questions, let me know."

Sarah sank down onto a log and Dean knelt beside her with his own hot dog. Wood smoke curled around them. Children laughed in the distance.

She stared into the fire, mesmerized by the flames that leapt around. She concentrated on the fire and tried not to think about anything beyond tonight. Her future would be here soon enough.

Dean was here tonight.

"So, what do you think?" Dean asked.

Sarah's lips were covered with marshmallow and the tiniest bit of chocolate. When she'd admitted that not only had she never cooked a hot dog over a fire, but she'd never had s'mores, Dean made another trip to the camp store for the chocolate bars, marshmallows and graham crackers.

"Heaven," Sarah replied, slowly licking the marshmallow from her lips.

But she didn't get it all and Dean couldn't resist leaning over and sweeping the corner of her mouth with his tongue. Then it seemed so natural to cover her lips with his.

So sweet. And it wasn't the leftover marshmallow that made it that way. It was Sarah and the little moan she made deep in her throat. And the way she leaned into the kiss, almost as if it had been her idea all along.

Her tongue tangled with his, deepening the kiss, heating him more than the fire they were sitting beside. He had to resist the urge to pull her onto his lap, right here in the middle of the campground in still way too much daylight. The sun couldn't set fast enough.

But there was something he had to do before he pulled Sarah into that tent and made love with her again. And again. There was some confessing he had to do. But how did he bring the subject up? *Oh, by the way, remember everything I told you about my life...?*

He slowly pulled away from her, his lips reluctantly leaving hers behind. Sarah stared at him for a moment, then looked up at the clear blue sky. He followed her gaze. Streaks of pink and purple colored the horizon.

"What a perfect night," she said.

"Yeah." *Just suck it up and do it, Bastian.* "Uh, Sarah..."

"You know the woman I introduced you to today?" Sarah interrupted.

He was disgusted with himself when relief flooded him at the brief reprieve. "In the laundry room? Yeah."

"She and her husband travel all year round in their motor home. They don't even have a regular house."

"Yeah, there's a lot of full-time RVers out there."

She sighed and stared into the fire. "I envy them. What a

great way to live. One adventure after another."

Dean looked at her sharply. He could hear that touch of desperation in her voice again. She still yearned for adventure. But why? He'd known from the beginning that there had to be more to Sarah's story than what she'd told him, but he hadn't wanted to push it. He thought she would tell him eventually. But she hadn't.

Maybe it was time to push a little. He ignored the little voice that reminded him he was only postponing his own confession time.

"Are you okay, Sarah?" Dean asked her. He'd turned on his counselor voice, soft and smooth. "Is there something you want to talk about?"

She turned away from the fire and looked at him. "I'm sitting here thinking that I haven't done anything with my life." Her laugh was a short, bitter bark. "It's not even a life. It's just an existence." She swung her gaze back to the fire. "A boring existence."

He took her hand. "You finished school. You have a job." He grimaced. Stated like that, it did sound pretty boring.

"Yeah, wow, I finished high school. I never even ventured into college. I work day after boring day in a bank. I cash people's checks and deposit money. Nothing an ATM can't do."

"Why do you think your life is this way?" Dean asked softly.

Tears glistened in the firelight. "Because I was trying to be sensible. Security is important, right? A lot of people I know went to college, racked up enormous debt, and then couldn't get a job outside the fast food industry. I got a job at the bank right out of high school. I made money right off the bat. It seemed like the sensible thing to do."

Dean couldn't resist reaching out and catching a tear that ran down her cheek. "What would you rather be doing?"

Her sigh seemed to come from somewhere deep within her soul. "That's the sad part. I don't even know. Until recently I didn't even know I wanted something else."

"Well, let's try an easier question," Dean said. "Why did you want to take this trip?"

She tilted her chin up in a little expression of defiance. Or maybe pride. "So I could look back and say 'I did this.' I took a trip across the country on a motorcycle. That's not something everybody gets to do."

"No, it's not."

Her smile was a little shaky. "Thank you for taking me."

"You're welcome."

"How long have you had your bike?"

Dean recognized the change of subject, but decided he wouldn't push her anymore tonight. "This bike? I got it a little over a year ago. But I got my first motorcycle when I was sixteen. It was a piece of junk. I rebuilt it in the shed out back. It was a way to get out of the house. Away from my dad."

"I remember you riding up and down the street on that bike," Sarah said. "It was so loud some of the little kids would cover their ears when you rode by."

"I loved that bike." Dean said.

"I loved watching you on that bike," Sarah told him. "You were the image of sex and freedom."

"You thought that back then?" Dean couldn't keep the shock out of his voice.

She laughed, her eyes bright, the tears gone. "Well, maybe not in those words back then. But those are the words I'd use now."

"Sex and freedom," Dean repeated, watching the light from the fire dance in her eyes. "I like that."

132

"Do you get to ride much when you're on tour?"

He'd been just about to reach out and tangle his fingers in her hair. He stopped short. "What?"

"When you're on tour, working, do you get to ride your motorcycle much?"

Oh, hell. Here it was, the perfect opening to tell her the truth. How did he start? "Um...well...I..."

Before he could stutter anymore, she leaned toward him and kissed him. Tenderly. Sweetly.

"I'm sorry, I've wanted to do that for ages. I couldn't wait any longer." She cradled his face in her hands and looked into his eyes, her expression suddenly very intense. "We only have a couple more nights, don't we?"

"If we stick to the expressway, probably only one more night after tonight."

She nodded, not saying a word.

"Or did you want to go off the beaten path again tomorrow?"

She shook her head slowly. "No, it's time to go through to Denver. I know you have to be getting back to work. And I have things I have to do too."

Why was he disappointed? Shouldn't he be glad to get this trip over with? To start the next phase of his life? But would Sarah be there with him?

Not unless he 'fessed up. And soon.

She leaned over and kissed him again, with more passion than he'd ever felt before in a mere kiss, and he met her urgency with some of his own. She gathered him to her and he tried to remember why he didn't want to carry her to the tent this very moment.

Oh, yeah, confession time. He tried to pull away from her.

133

"Sarah, wait."

"Shhh," she said, her lips roaming over his face. "No more talking tonight."

"But I have something I need to tell you," Dean said. At least, he meant to say that, he really did, but she was eating him alive and he didn't think the words ever made it past his lips.

She jumped to her feet. "Make love to me now," she said, her voice low and passionate. She grabbed his hands and pulled him to his feet. He would have followed her to the tent in an instant except for that look of desperation on her face. The one he first saw the day she'd come to beg for a ride to California.

He pulled back from her and grasped her shoulders. "Tell me what's wrong."

"Nothing's wrong that a little sex won't cure," she told him, pulling his shirt out from the waistband of his jeans. "You've got me so hot and bothered I can't think straight. Let's not talk any more tonight. I wouldn't know what I was saying."

He wasn't thinking straight either, because he couldn't think of a single reason why he shouldn't spend the rest of the evening making sweet love to Sarah. He let her pull his T-shirt over his head and she tossed it over her shoulder with a grin. She reached for him and pulled him into her arms. The evening air brushed across his back, cooling his skin in the wake of her hot, roaming fingers.

He captured her lips in the gathering darkness, drinking in her sweetness. Could she read his love in the tenderness of his kiss? Could she tell he wasn't the wandering man she thought he was?

Laughing children ran by, reminding Dean that they were standing in the middle of their campsite, their kisses illuminated by the campfire and the setting sun. He reluctantly pulled away. "Let me douse the campfire and we can turn in."

Sarah nodded. She turned around to glance at the fire and a look of horror crossed her face. Dean followed her gaze and saw his T-shirt halfway in the fire, burning brightly along with the firewood.

He laughed and dumped the rest of his root beer over the flames.

Chapter Nine

The rain started falling sometime during the night. By the time Dean stirred in Sarah's arms, the ground was soggy beneath her. He opened his eyes and smiled at her. Her heart stumbled in her chest.

She loved him, and for the very first time she let herself feel the joy. How lucky she was to have taken this trip. She could have lived her whole life and never experienced true love. She might never have known a man like Dean.

It was times like this that she could almost believe in happily ever after. Almost believe that if Dean was ever ready to settle down with one woman, she was the one.

Then she remembered Mrs. Cheney and her quick descent into the MS nightmare. How likely was it that the same thing would happen to Sarah? She wished now that she'd read all that literature she'd been given. When she had heard the diagnosis last week—was it only last week?—she didn't want to listen to any more. Her confusing variety of symptoms had plagued her off and on for more than a year. Just because it now had a name didn't mean she wanted anything to do with it.

She didn't want to know what to expect. She didn't want to worry about what to do to help control her symptoms. She certainly didn't want to hear she had to give herself shots in the thigh for the rest of her life.

Sarah knew enough to realize not everyone with MS progressed in the same way, but the chance was there that she could end up like Mrs. Cheney. Sarah had been given a life sentence, and while it might not be a death penalty, it sure killed every chance she had of living a normal life.

She didn't want to think about it.

Dean reached up and swept his fingertips gently across her cheek. "What are you thinking about so seriously?"

Sarah felt the frown wrinkling her forehead and consciously relaxed her face. She took a deep breath and shrugged her shoulders. "Just listening to the rain and thinking it won't be a fun ride today."

Dean sat up. "It'll be a little slower going, that's for sure. But we might run out of it as we go west."

Sarah nodded. She wanted to grab him, push him back down to the floor of the tent, and make love to him all day long. Forget about Denver. Forget about disabilities.

But she knew they had to get this trip over with before it would be even harder to say good-bye.

Who was she kidding? It was already going to hurt like hell.

The rain continued as they rushed to tear down camp and it didn't let up when they climbed on the Harley and took off toward Denver. Hot and soaking already, the rain suit seemed like a sauna to Sarah.

When she'd started out on this trip, the term adventure conjured up exciting and wonderful experiences. She never thought she'd be barreling down the highway, pummeled by driving rain that did nothing to relieve the mugginess in the heavy air.

The fatigue that usually hit her in the early afternoon struck sooner today. The heat was doing a number on her. She wrapped her limp and leaden arms around Dean and leaned heavily against his back.

Today, traveling by motorcycle wasn't fun or exhilarating. It was simply miserable.

Just when she thought it couldn't rain any harder, the skies opened up and pummeled them with sheets of water. At the next overpass, Dean pulled the bike off the road beneath the shelter of the bridge.

Sarah followed his example and stiffly got off the bike and leaned back against the concrete embankment. They took off their helmets and, for a few minutes, silently watched the rain.

"I couldn't see," Dean said finally, scrubbing his hand over his face.

"I don't know how you got us this far," Sarah told him. "You did a great job handling the bike."

"It's hard work just to keep it on the road," he said. "Let's hope it lets up soon."

Sarah nodded and stared at the water flowing off the bridge. "It's like standing behind a waterfall."

"I did that once," Dean said.

"You did? Stood behind a real waterfall?"

Dean nodded. "I was out on the bike in the middle of nowhere. I stopped for lunch by a creek and that's when I heard it. You know, the sound of falling water. It was easy to find. I just followed the creek toward the sound. I could see a trail where other people had gone up to this ledge behind the falls. It was a long climb up, but it was worth it. The view was awesome." He looked at her and smiled. "I'll take you there sometime."

"Sure," she said vaguely, knowing it would never happen. She couldn't find any enthusiasm to put in her voice. "That would be great." Then she closed her eyes so she didn't have to see the confused look on Dean's face.

A few minutes later, he said, "It looks a little better. Let's head for the next rest area. I'm starving."

She hadn't noticed any change in the force of the rain, but she nodded and put her helmet back on. She followed him back through the falling water and onto the Harley.

Dean pulled the bike into the next rest area they came to. They ran through the rain toward the protection of the building. Sarah's run was more of a limping hop, but she managed to keep up with Dean.

"Not quite what you had in mind when you signed on for this trip, is it?" Dean asked, as they shook the excess water from their hair and clothing.

"No, I have to admit I was thinking more along the lines of sunshine and gentle breezes."

Dean laughed. "Well, just like anything, you have to take the bad with the good." He turned and headed toward the small food court.

Sarah followed, hoping some food would give her much needed energy. Her brain felt fuzzy too. What did he say? Why did she have the feeling it was something important?

Whatever it was, it was gone. Sarah bought her meal and joined Dean at a little table in a corner of the dining area. She sighed and took a long drink of coffee.

"You okay?" Dean asked, looking at her with concern in his eyes.

She nodded. "Just tired. The storm woke me up last night." That much was true. But once the thunder and lightning disturbed her sleep, thoughts of a future without Dean wouldn't let her fall back to sleep either.

Don't go there. She had to think about something else. Like how sexy he looked with his long, damp hair and a hint of beard shadowing his face. Like how the slightest touch of his fingers could send quivers of need racing along her skin. Like how she'd never get enough of seeing him and touching him...

Don't go there.

She pasted a bright smile on her face and tried to think of something, anything to talk about, to get her mind off the longing in her heart. "So, Dean. I'm willing to bet this isn't the worst weather you've ever taken your bike through."

Dean laughed and chugged half his glass of orange juice. "The hailstorm in Oklahoma would be the worst," he said, setting the glass back down. He rubbed his arm as if he was remembering, but his smile was still in place. "Never again."

Sarah winced at the thought. "Ow."

"Yeah." Dean stared at her for a moment and the smile faded from his face. "You are so beautiful."

She knew what she had to look like. Something close to a drowned rat. The tenderness in Dean's voice, however, actually made her feel beautiful. "Dean..."

"I have an idea," he said, a sparkle in his eye, the smile back on his lips. "What do you say we stop at a hotel tonight?"

Soft mattress. Private bath. "Really?"

"Any campground we find is going to have had all this rain. I'd rather sleep in a warm, dry bed, how about you?"

"Oh, that sounds wonderful."

"Besides, it's going to be our last night," Dean said.

As if she needed to be reminded. The eggs she'd swallowed sank in her stomach like a rock.

He lowered his voice to a near whisper. "I'd like to make love to you in a real bed for once." He stroked her hand with his finger. "Soft pillows. Soft mattress. Soft Sarah."

There were those quivers again. Sarah could picture it so clearly. She and Dean lying beneath sheets instead of sleeping bags. A real mattress instead of the hard ground beneath their bodies. A hot shower they could share when the lovemaking was over.

If this was their last night together, they might as well go out in style.

Dean's mind was on the night to come—a quiet hotel room, Sarah in his arms, their bodies coming together as one. So he didn't even see it coming. He'd angled his face against the pouring rain and was checking out his bike, not looking at Sarah, as they crossed the rest area parking lot.

It was the blast of the horn that got his attention. That and the squealing tires. He whipped his head around and saw the red pickup truck pulling a boat trailer behind it. The truck was stopped in the middle of the parking lot and a man jumped out of the truck into the downpour.

Where was Sarah? He couldn't see her anywhere. He spun around, pushing his wet hair out of his face, but she wasn't behind him either. Dean started running for the pickup before he even consciously allowed himself to fear that Sarah was under the wheels of that huge vehicle.

She lay sprawled in front of the truck, motionless on the wet pavement. Dean reached her in an instant, his heart in his throat. By the time he knelt beside her in a large puddle, she groaned and started to push herself up with her arms.

"Are you all right?" he asked, his voice coming out like a croak. He curbed the urge to pull her into his arms. He first ran his hands along her soaking wet body, checking for broken bones. "What happened, honey? Were you hit?"

"I fell," Sarah said shakily. She sat up on the pavement, the tears from her eyes mingling with the rain streaming from her hair. She looked up at the middle-aged man who hovered over them, rain dripping from his handle-bar mustache. "I'm so sorry."

"You scared the daylights out of me, little lady," he said. "Are you hurt?"

Sarah shook her head. "I'm fine."

"Are you sure?" Dean asked. She nodded, but didn't meet his eye. He gently helped her to her feet, then kept his arm around her waist. He couldn't let her go. He had to hold her, reassure himself that she was all right.

"Embarrassed is more like it," she said. Her body trembled against his.

"Well, I'm just glad I got good brakes," the man said, wiping the rain off his face.

"Me, too." Dean said. He stepped away from Sarah long enough to shake the man's hand. "Well, we'd all better get out of the rain. Thanks for being so alert."

"Take care of her, young man," the pickup driver said. With a wave, he hopped back into his truck and pulled away slowly.

"Let's get back inside," Dean said. He kept his arm around her, holding her tightly against him. "Be careful. I didn't realize how slippery this wet pavement is."

He was just starting to understand how much Sarah meant to him. He could have lost her today, before he ever really had her in his life. Tonight he was going to remedy that. They were going to have dinner at the hotel dining room and he was going to ask her to marry him. The idea of marriage didn't frighten him at all anymore, but the thought of losing Sarah scared him to death.

All he had to worry about was getting there in one piece, and, of course, confessing to Sarah that he'd been lying to her since they'd met again in the bank in Buffalo.

When they reached a bench inside the building, he sat down, bringing Sarah with him. They were wringing wet, water running off their hair and saturated rain suits. He wished they were already at the hotel where they could dry off with big towels and warm up in a soft bed.

He stood up. He couldn't think about that now.

"Sarah, I'm going to run out to the bike and grab the saddlebags. There'll be something there we can use to dry off with."

Sarah nodded and looked down at her hands in her lap. Dean followed her gaze and saw her scraped palms, dirty and bloody. He dropped to his knees beside her.

"Aw, honey. Let me look at those hands."

She pulled her hands away. "They're fine." She stood up. "What's the sense of drying off? We're going to get soaked again the minute we go back out there."

"Yeah, you're right. At least go clean off your hands."

Sarah nodded. "Okay, be right back."

Dean dropped a kiss on the tip of her nose and reluctantly let her out of his sight.

Sarah hoped the tears streaming down her face would be mistaken for the water still running from her hair. Women walking into the restroom stared at her curiously. She must have looked a sight.

She had to stop crying before she went back out to Dean, but the tears wouldn't stop. So many emotions bombarded her as she stood at the sink, rinsing dirt and blood out of her scraped palms. Embarrassment, exhaustion, relief, regret. Fear.

She'd be having nightmares about that truck for the rest of her life. Sarah had only to close her eyes to see the huge tires and chrome grill only inches from her head. She'd hear those squealing tires forever. How had she ended up on the pavement in front of a pickup truck?

It wasn't fair. She was tired, but she thought she'd been walking very carefully. The whole thing had happened so fast, she could hardly recall the details. She remembered feeling a little off balance and she might have caught her toe. That was probably all she needed on top of the wet pavement to send her flying in front of a moving vehicle.

She shivered again, but not from the chill of the air conditioning on her wet skin. Would she have to worry for the rest of her life?

Sarah managed to get her tears and emotions under control before she left the restroom. Her heartbeat slowed to something close to normal. She didn't get hurt, that was the important thing. The journey was ending soon. She would be back in Buffalo before she knew it. She'd gotten behind on her journal entries, but she'd soon have lots of time to catch up. She had to put today's experience in perspective and chalk it up as part of the adventure.

She couldn't let it spoil her last night with Dean.

A hotel room had never seemed so luxurious. Clean sheets. Soft bed. Hot water.

This time, Sarah didn't have to share a shower room with screeching little girls or pokey old women. Just one sexy bad boy who snuck in when she wasn't looking.

A hot shower had been first on Sarah's agenda after they checked in. She peeled her clothes off, left them where they lay on the floor and turned on the water, hot and hard. The water felt like heaven, cascading over her cold, tired body. How long would the hot water hold out? She could stay right here for hours.

The steam had begun rising around her when Dean slipped around the shower curtain and joined her, a mischievous grin on his face. A nervous tickle started deep in her stomach and danced up into her throat. She'd never shared a shower before. He seemed to fill the small space with his hard, muscular body. To give him room, she stepped back under the stream of the showerhead.

She could almost imagine they were standing under the waterfall Dean told her about. She might never be able to climb behind a waterfall with him, but this was the next best thing. The hot water caressed her skin and might have relaxed her if she hadn't been nearly shivering in anticipation. So far he'd only stood there, melting her with his gaze.

Of course, she couldn't take her eyes off of him, either. Not off his tight body or his rigid arousal. The tanned muscles in his arms tensed as he made loose fists with his hands. Was he fighting the urge to touch her? He hadn't made a move toward her, but she knew if he didn't touch her soon, she was going to make a move of her own. Or dissolve into a puddle and wash down the drain.

The dark desire in Dean's eyes nearly made her knees give out. She placed her hand on the ceramic tile wall to steady herself. "Dean..." she whispered. "Please..." She didn't know what she was begging for, but Dean stepped forward as if he knew.

"Here," he said. He took her wrists in his hands and lifted her arms above her head. He curled her fingers over the pipe at the top of the showerhead. "Don't let go."

Sarah clutched the metal with her hands, the water from the showerhead cascading over her shoulder. Without a sound, she watched Dean work up a handful of lather from the tiny bar of hotel soap. She stood there, completely vulnerable. Tingles of arousal were already bouncing through her body. Moisture pooled within her and Dean had yet to touch anything but her hands.

"Beautiful Sarah," he said, and finally touched her the way she'd been longing for him to do.

Her body sang with awareness when Dean rubbed his soapy hands along her arms and across her throat. She gasped when he lingered on her breasts, kneading their fullness, teasing the peaks through the thick lather.

She itched to touch him too and started to let go of the showerhead. Dean's dark gaze met hers and he shook his head slowly. "No. Not yet. Let me do this for you."

He slid his slick hands back up her arms and clasped her hands once again above the showerhead. She dropped her head back and gave up the control she always felt she needed. She held on tightly and simply let him do what he wanted with her. Trusting him to know where she needed to go. Trusting herself to let him take her there.

He swept his hands lazily along her body, cupping her breasts again, rolling her nipples between his slick fingers. As he dove lower, he skimmed her ribs, brushing her quivering stomach. He gradually reached lower and lower with each sensual caress. Finally, he stretched one hand lower still and slid it between her legs. His soapy fingers slipped around the little nub of desire. Her knees threatened to give out when waves of sensation rolled through her. She grasped the shower head to keep from falling. She couldn't stop the moan from escaping her lips or the gasp that followed in its wake.

"That's it," he murmured as he kept up the delicious stroking between her legs. "Let go. Let me see you let go, Sarah. Let me see you go."

And then she was tumbling over the waterfalls. Free falling. Spiraling back to earth. Landing in his arms.

He gathered her to him as she landed and she dropped her hands to hold onto his shoulders for support. The spray from the shower washed over them.

Her body was still riding the ebbing waves when Dean captured her lips with his. His lips were wet from the shower and from his own desire, and when they slid across her mouth, Sarah drank deeply.

Gradually, Sarah seemed to gain control of her body again. She felt sated and energetic all at the same time. She shook her hands out for a moment, before she leaned over and grabbed the bar of soap.

"My turn."

She thought she'd touched him before. She thought she knew what his body felt like. His skin was a different texture beneath her fingers with the layer of soap between them. His muscles were somehow smoother, the definition more pronounced. She slid her soapy hands around his hips and cupped his tight buttocks, bringing him closer against her.

Then she took his hard, smooth erection into her soapy hands and worked up a lather that grew thick and smooth. The ridges and veins seemed more pronounced here too. She stroked him slowly, drawing her hands up the hard length of him over and over again.

"Sarah..." he groaned, her name sounding strangled as it came from his throat.

"Hold on," she murmured, a smile breaking free. She repeated his words back at him. "Let me do this for you."

"If you do much more of that, I won't be able to last."

She kept up the stroking, liking the idea of driving him over the edge. Finally, Dean groaned out loud. He grabbed her by the waist and pulled her under the flowing water with him. When the shower rinsed all the soap off, Dean pushed her up against the wall of the shower stall. He slid his hand between her thighs. She was wet and ready for him.

He rubbed his hard arousal along her slick cleft. "So much for finally making love with you in a real bed."

"Hey, we've got all night," she said, spreading her legs and opening for him. Cooling water from the showerhead washed over them as he slid into her.

They fit perfectly together. Didn't she know that already? She matched him thrust for thrust, breath for breath. Heart for heart.

If only he was someone who wanted to settle down, have a family, love one woman.

If only she were someone with a promising future, able to take on the responsibilities of family, be an equal partner, not a burden, to the man she loved.

Take care of her, that pickup driver had said to Dean. Sarah wanted to scream in frustration. She didn't want to have to be taken care of.

Besides, Dean didn't stick around anywhere long enough to take care of anything.

Sarah hugged Dean tighter, bringing him deeper inside her. She wanted it harder, stronger, wilder. She wanted her mind wiped clean of everything but this moment. This man.

Dean slid his hand between their slick bodies and, with one brush of his finger, touched off another wave of spasms. He joined her with his climax, clasping her to him, rocking her body against his. She didn't want to think anymore tonight. She just wanted to feel.

"I can't believe you had that dress packed in the saddlebag," Dean said.

Sarah laughed. She sounded as much like an angel as she looked.

"It's made of one of those fabrics that roll up into a little ball and never wrinkle," she told him. "I packed it in case we went to a nice restaurant or something."

He stared at Sarah as if he'd never seen her before. The pale pink dress wrapped around her body in ways that made him jealous. She wore a little bit of makeup that she'd tucked away as well, giving her eyes a sultry look he'd never expected and a rosy shine to her lips. Her bare legs teased him beneath the hem of the soft skirt.

"As soon as I find my sandals, I'll be ready for dinner," she told him. She bent over the saddlebag lying on top of the dresser and began to dig through the contents.

Dean longed to reach out and caress that shapely behind. Instead, he curled his fingers into his palms and shoved his hands into the pockets of the khaki pants from which Sarah had been able to iron most of the wrinkles.

He couldn't touch her again. Not until he came clean. He didn't deserve to have her in his arms again until he admitted his lies and told her the truth. He hoped she might return his love, but how could she when she didn't even know who he really was?

He'd tell her over dinner tonight. He'd make sure they had to sit across from each other at a big, wide table. Far enough away from each other that their knees wouldn't bump and their feet couldn't brush.

He simply wasn't able to keep his head on straight when he touched her. Or when he was near enough to her to smell that sweetness that had nothing to do with perfumes or colognes. Looking at her wasn't a big help in the concentration department, either, but he wasn't about to close his eyes. In fact, he was going into this with his eyes wide open.

He'd already crossed the room until he was only a breath away from her. She turned around with the sandals in one hand and rubbed her thumb across his scruffy chin. He hadn't bothered to shave on the trip. "You look so sexy like this."

He ran his gaze over her body. "Talk about sexy."

"Don't look at me that way," she said, laughter in her voice.

He'd already taken his hands out of his pockets. All he had to do was reach out his arm. "What way?"

"Like you want to have me for dinner."

Was he that transparent? He liked to think he was a stronger man, but he took the final step and gathered her into his arms. "Well, now that you mention it…"

She sank into him for a moment, then laughed and stepped away. He reluctantly let her go. "Come on, Dean. I'm starved. Can't we have dinner first?"

Dinner. Right. They had to have dinner first. He was glad someone had her head on straight. He shoved his hands in his pockets again and backed away.

He watched her slip her bare feet into a pair of hardly-there sandals. He swallowed hard, trying to moisten his suddenly dry throat. He couldn't think about getting her in that big bed. He had to concentrate. She deserved the truth and he was going to give it to her.

Sarah took his hand as they walked down the long hall to the dining room. Although Dean knew it wasn't a good idea to touch her, he couldn't pull away. It would be okay. They'd get a big table and he'd get the confession out of the way before the main course.

They paused at the door of the dining room and the hostess hurried over to them. Dean got his first peek at the dining room and his optimism sank in his stomach. The place was crawling with people. Still, he asked for a roomy table for the two of them.

"I'm sorry, sir, I'm afraid I don't have any large tables available," the hostess said. "However, I do have a cozy little table for two back in the corner."

Chapter Ten

It was a cozy little table all right, but Sarah didn't mind at all. Her knees rubbed against Dean's beneath the long white tablecloth. The delightful friction sent sparks dancing through her body.

As she traced the length of his fingers, she remembered the feel of them stroking her body. All she wanted to do was touch him. It was crazy. Less than an hour ago they'd made love, but she ached to do it all over again.

Not exactly what anyone, especially herself, would have expected from Sensible Sarah. She'd always been the good girl. She'd never even considered doing anything unconventional. Who'd have thought she'd be hundreds of miles from home craving sex with a man she had no future with?

She'd left Sensible Sarah far behind in Buffalo. Who was this Sarah? Who was she now?

She stroked Dean's skin with fingers that grew more numb as the day went by. The numbness in her hands was the first symptom that sent her to the first of many doctors over a year ago. Before long she was bothered by blurred vision and the problems with her balance. Her vision had straightened out for the moment, but in its place was the foot that seemed to trip her up when she least expected it.

Whoever Sarah was now, she wasn't a woman who could travel around the country with Dean like Marge Berrey did with her husband. Sarah didn't want to tie anyone down to the future she had in store, least of all Dean.

What on earth was she worrying about? Dean didn't want one woman to spend his life with anyway. He didn't want to settle down. His life was on the road, traveling with a rock and roll band, partying with the little chickies who followed them around.

Did he have a favorite? A pretty little thing he looked for after each concert? Someone who warmed his bed on a regular basis and kept him from being lonely?

Jealousy, pure and simple, flared within Sarah. She knew she had no right to feel jealous, but she couldn't control the bitterness that burned deep in her stomach.

She looked up from his hand to find him watching her. A smile slowly spread across his face and melted the tension within her.

"You get prettier every day," he said softly. He captured her hand in his and squeezed it gently. Her face grew warm in response to his words. "You're the most beautiful woman in the place. How did I get so lucky to be here with you?"

Sarah caught her breath. What made him say something like that? Did he mean it? Was it just a line he threw to the girl of the moment? Did he say that to the groupie who shared his bed on the road?

She told herself again that she had no right to be jealous, so she did her best to kick that bitter mood. She hoped her smile didn't look forced as she said lightly, "You didn't think that when I first asked you to take me with you."

"Well, you shocked the hell out of me." He surprised her by reaching out and brushing his fingers against her cheek. His touch was like a feather. "I didn't know what to think when you all but begged me to take you with me." He chuckled. "But I'm glad I said yes."

Soft ripples of awareness swept over her body, teasing her with what she couldn't keep.

"But you like to travel alone," she said, with more than a touch of desperation. She knew he didn't need to be told what he did and didn't like to do, but it seemed as if he needed to be reminded. "You told me that on our first day out. Remember?"

He traced her lower lip with the tip of his finger and gazed at her with eyes steeped in sincerity. "Maybe I never had the right traveling companion before."

The sigh escaped her lips before she even realized it. Boy, he knew the right things to say.

Of course he did, she reminded herself. He'd had a lot of practice bestowing the right lines to women over the years.

Even as Sarah thought that, a part of her wanted to believe that he hadn't been feeding her a bunch of lines. A part of her *did* believe it. She knew Dean hadn't been telling her only what he thought she wanted to hear. He'd been honest with her. Honest and funny and sensitive.

No wonder she'd fallen in love with him.

But that was a secret she'd hold close to her heart for the rest of her life.

She'd never even bothered to look at the menu, so when the waitress stopped to take their order, she saved time by ordering what Dean did, a steak with baked potato and tossed salad. A little while ago she'd been starving. She thought it had been for food, but she was wrong. She hungered for what only Dean could give her.

She slowly slid her foot up the calf of his leg and smiled at the surprised expression that flashed across his face. Surprise that was quickly replaced with desire. She liked knowing she had that kind of power over him. She hoped they could get this meal over with quickly, so they could try out the big bed in their room.

"Thank you for taking me on this trip," Sarah told him after the waitress left their table. After all, this was their last night together and she was afraid she might forget to thank him tomorrow. "It has been a once-in-a-lifetime journey."

"Once in a lifetime? What are you talking about?" he asked. "You can go on lots more trips. You could learn to ride a bike yourself, if you wanted to."

If only she could. If only she could be the woman Dean thought she was. She'd never be the right traveling companion for him. Sarah shrugged and looked away, hoping he wouldn't see the truth in her eyes.

When she didn't reply, Dean said, "So, tell me. What's a woman who's never traveled before, and never plans to again, doing with a dress designed for packing?"

"She was always hoping." The words came out of Sarah's mouth before she thought about it. She immediately wished she could take them back. Oh, God, what would Dean think of her now? Poor Sarah. A pitiful woman, who sat at home and dreamed about a life she would never dare live.

And now that she'd dared, it was too late.

"Why just hoping?" he asked, his voice low and smooth. He looked her in the eye as if he cared about her answer. "Why haven't you gone out and traveled if that's what you wanted to do?"

The waitress came with their salads and Sarah waited until she was gone to respond. She knew he'd never understand, but she'd try to explain. "Because it wasn't sensible."

155

"Sensible?"

Sarah speared a cherry tomato, popped it in her mouth, and chewed it thoughtfully before she answered him. "I was the oldest child and my parents expected a lot from me." She could still feel the weight of their expectations on her shoulders. "I had to set an example for my sisters. I had to be the sensible one. I had to be the good girl."

She shook her head, certain Dean wouldn't be able to relate. "Oh, how I would have loved to play hooky from school, just once. But I never dared. I would have never been able to bear the look of disappointment in my parents' eyes."

She stopped talking and looked away. She couldn't believe she said that out loud. She shoved a forkful of salad in her mouth, not even tasting it. She'd never admitted that to anyone before. What did it mean, she wondered, that she admitted it to Dean, the consummate bad boy?

"Honey, I can understand parents' expectations. My parents expected something totally different from me, but I felt it all the same." He set down his fork and seemed to study her face. What did he see there? "But what does that have to do with not traveling?"

She knew he wouldn't understand. He never knew what it was like to be expected to set the good example. He never knew what it was like to grow up as Sensible Sarah. Her parents had actually called her that, for Heaven's sake. She was their Sensible Sarah. How could she not feel the responsibility to live up to that?

"It would have been frivolous," she told him. "It would have meant I wasn't happy with my life the way it was. It would have cost money." She sighed. "It would not have been sensible."

"Suzy went to Europe after graduation, didn't she?" Dean asked.

Sarah nodded. She'd been so excited for her youngest sister's chance to tour Europe during college. Excited and yet so envious.

"But she studied languages," Sarah said, for some reason feeling the need to defend her sister. "Did you know she's an interpreter in New York City now?"

Dean nodded. "I heard. Sharon doesn't live in Buffalo either, does she?"

"She moved to Florida after she married Billy Lyle." Sarah had wished her all the best, even as she yearned to follow. But Sarah had never even gone down to visit them, not once in the two years since they'd been gone.

She'd worked so hard to be the good girl. The Sensible Sarah her parents had wanted her to be. She'd never thought about the fact that her sisters apparently hadn't felt that same need.

"Hey, wait a minute." She pushed her salad plate away. "How do you know what's been going on with my sisters?" she asked.

"Terry keeps up on the news. She gives me the scoop on the old neighborhood."

Sarah couldn't help but wonder if he'd kept up on news of her as well. However, since she'd never done anything newsworthy in her entire boring, predictable life, there would have been no news for Terry to pass on. Had he ever wondered what happened to her?

"So you and Terry buried the hatchet," she said, instead of asking what she really wanted to know. "I'm glad."

Dean shrugged. "It was our dad. He liked to pit the two of us against each other, thought it was funny or something. Once we got away from him, we got along fine. She and her husband, Joe, own a two-family house in Denver. I live upstairs over them."

"It must be nice to have a place to come home to when you're not on the road."

Dean frowned, but right then the waitress came with their meals and Sarah didn't get a chance to ask him why.

He had to tell her the truth. It tore Dean up inside to have her thinking he was still a wanderer. Still a womanizer. He had to find a way to tell her he wasn't on the road. That he wanted to settle down, and he wanted to settle down with her.

At the moment, however, he was trying to cut his steak with a dull knife and not react to her foot sliding up and down his leg. When she did that he couldn't think straight. His pants tightened at the crotch and he started remembering how fine she'd felt in the shower not too long ago. How her wet, slick skin had slithered along his. How her hot, moist mouth had tasted while the water had showered over them.

Her foot slid farther up his leg. It took all the control he had not to jump out of his seat when she reached his hard and swollen crotch. He shot a glance from his plate to the innocent look on her face. Then, without breaking eye contact, Sarah slowly licked the steak sauce off her fork with long sweeps of her tongue.

Now he didn't even care about his steak and the damn knife that wouldn't cut it. All he cared about was Sarah. Touching Sarah. Needing her. Loving her. He dropped his knife onto the plate and took her hand in his.

She looked up at him and smiled.

That smile. It was all he could do to stop himself from jumping up and pulling her into his arms.

"I love you." The words burst out of his mouth before he

realized he was even thinking them.

The smile dropped from her face. "What?"

His good mood slipped a notch or two. What could he say to bring that smile back? Didn't women want to hear those three little words? "I love you, Sarah. I've loved you for a while now. I thought you'd want to know."

She pulled her hand from his grasp and shook her head. "No. You can't."

Well, this certainly wasn't the way he'd wanted the conversation to go. "I wouldn't think you'd be so surprised. We've been making love these last few nights."

Her voice was bitter as she said, "You know as well as I do that you can have sex without being in love."

An older couple at the table next to them turned around to stare. This wasn't the place to be having this conversation. Dean lowered his voice. "I never thought of what we did as merely having sex. I was making love with you. I thought you were doing the same."

If he didn't know better, he'd think there was a spark of sadness in her eyes. Sadness that was replaced with fear. She looked down at her plate of uneaten food and didn't say anything.

"Well, I love you, Sarah Austin. I've never felt for anyone else the way I feel for you."

"Oh, I get it," she said, her face twisting into a smirk. "This is what you say to all your women, isn't it? Tell me, do you believe it at the time, Dean? Does it make you feel better to tell them that? Does it ease your conscience to think you are actually in love with the woman you're sleeping with at the moment?"

The first stab of concern speared his stomach. Maybe what

he thought was so simple, wasn't at all.

"I've never been in love before, Sarah. Never. And there certainly haven't been anywhere near as many women as you seem to think." He closed his eyes for a minute, praying for the right words to come. When he opened them again, she still had that skeptical look on her face. "I'm a little confused here. I kinda thought you'd be happy to hear that I've fallen in love with you. Care to share why you're so upset?"

She rolled her eyes, as if the answer was obvious.

Dean held up his hand before she could say anything. How could he have been so dense? He knew what the problem was. The moment of truth had come.

"You don't have to say anything," he said quickly. "I know why you don't believe me. Hell, I wouldn't believe me either. It's all been a misunderstanding, Sarah. Once I explain, it will all make sense and I hope you'll see it in your heart to forgive me."

She frowned. "Forgive you for what?"

He took a deep breath. He wished she had a little more compassionate look on her face. How did he start to tell her the truth without making her shut down completely? "When I was growing up, I always envied your life."

He could tell that took her by surprise. "*My* life? I had a boring life. Nothing ever happened to me. And what does this have to do with...?"

He put his hand on hers and was relieved that she didn't pull it away. "Bear with me, please. I used to sit out on the curb sometimes and watch your family when you were outside. Did you know that?"

She shook her head and frowned again.

"Not like a peeping Tom or anything," he said, quickly. "But just because I liked watching a happy family. I could almost pretend I was a part of it. I'm sure you know that ours was anything but."

"Not while I was growing up," she admitted. "Terry would come over and play with me, but she never invited me over to your house. I never understood why back then."

At least she wasn't glaring at him anymore. Maybe if he could keep her talking, she wouldn't shut him out again.

"I still remember one hot summer day," Dean went on, "when your Dad got out the hose and chased you and your sisters around your front yard."

"Yeah, we loved it when he did that," she said. "We pretended we wanted him to stop. But we never did."

"And on Halloween, while I was out smashing pumpkins and wrapping cars with toilet paper, your Mom walked you and your sisters around to all the houses to trick or treat."

"Our car never got wrapped in toilet paper."

"I only did it to people I didn't like."

"Oh."

"My childhood was nothing like yours, Sarah." He laughed, a bitter bark that sounded harsh even to his own ears. "That's an understatement. It was hell."

"I'm so sorry. I didn't know."

He didn't want her pity; he wanted her to understand. He knew she still thought of him as the rebellious bad boy, and he'd done nothing to correct her. No wonder she didn't believe his declaration of love.

"Despite what you may think you know about me," he said, "I'm ready to settle down. I want to have a family like you had growing up."

"What?"

Dean tried to laugh off the stunned look she had on her

161

face. "Yeah, it shocked the hell out of me too when I realized it."

She just stared at him and repeated, "What?"

She didn't have to look *that* shocked.

"It's all your fault, Sarah. You did it to me. You changed me forever." He ran his fingers through his hair, trying to find the right words to say to get her to lose that stunned expression. "Something's been missing from my life for a long time. It had always been missing. But it wasn't until I met you that I figured it out. I know you think you know the type of guy I am, but you don't. I want it all, Sarah. The wife, the kids, the white picket fence."

Wasn't she supposed to start being relieved now? Or was it that hard to believe that he could want to settle down? Did Sarah see something in him that he couldn't see? A cold sweat washed over him.

"I'm kidding myself, right?" he said, the bitterness clear in his voice. "Yeah, what kind of father would I be? What kind of husband? Look at the role model I had."

"Oh, no, Dean," she protested. "That wasn't what I was thinking at all."

"My father was an abusive drunk. My mother was a worn-out woman long before she got cancer. I wouldn't know what to do with a wife and kids if I had them."

"You'd love them," Sarah said, grabbing his hands. "I know you would. You have a good heart. You'd make a wonderful husband and father."

It irked him that he needed the reassurance, but he had desperately wanted to hear those words from her. The bitterness instantly disappeared, leaving a warm glow behind. He hadn't been wrong about her.

"Marry me, Sarah. Be my wife. I want to spend the rest of

my life with you. We can raise children and ride Harleys together."

Sarah gasped and dropped his hands like they burned her. She pushed back her chair, the legs screeching against the tile floor. Her face seemed to drain of color before his eyes. "You can't mean that."

"Sarah?"

Her gaze bounced all over the room, but she didn't look at him. "You're on the road all year with a rock band. How can you hope to raise a family?"

He took a deep breath. "I don't travel with a rock band."

Now she was looking at him. "What? What are you saying?"

He sighed. "I'm not a roadie for Aerosmith. I only did it for one summer during college. I'm a counselor for troubled teens in Denver."

"You lied?" She stood up and threw her napkin down on the table. "You lied to me?"

The stricken look on her face was more than he could bear. "Try to understand," he went on, feeling desperate now, knowing the future he'd envisioned with her was slipping through his fingers. "You wanted an adventure. I thought that's who you wanted me to be."

"You're right," he thought he heard her say before she turned and ran away.

Everyone in the restaurant was staring at them. Dean tried to follow her, but the waitress stopped him with the bill. By the time he'd taken care of it, Sarah was gone.

Chapter Eleven

Sarah burst into the lobby. Where to go? He'd check their room first, and she needed some time alone before she saw him again. How did it all go so wrong? How could she have known Dean would be everything she ever wanted?

Why did she still want what she couldn't have?

Her unsteady balance threatened to send her to the floor. Her body shook like it was coming apart. She spied a stuffed chair in the corner of the lobby, inside a little niche. She sank gratefully into the chair and curled up against the nubby upholstery.

He wanted to marry her. That possibility had never occurred to her. Not Dean.

She thought she'd had it all figured out. A safe little fling with no strings attached. A lifetime of memories in a few short days.

Of course, she hadn't expected to fall in love with him either.

Dean deserved so much more than she could offer him. She had a lifetime of uncertainty ahead of her. She knew she might not end up in a wheelchair as quickly as Mrs. Cheney had, but she would become a burden sooner or later.

She couldn't do that to Dean. She had to let him go so he could find someone who could travel the country with him on a Harley and not trip and fall when she got off the bike. Someone who would still be healthy enough to travel with him for years down the road. Someone who could give him the children he wanted and the happy family life he desired.

No one would laugh at his children because their mother stumbled and fell down all the time.

She didn't realize she was crying until she tasted the salty tears. She didn't realize Dean had found her until he knelt in front of the chair.

"Sarah?" His handsome face was creased with concern. His eyes filled with confusion.

What could she say to him? She knew he didn't understand. How could he?

"I didn't mean to upset you," he said. "I know this all happened pretty fast. If you need time to think about it..."

"No, Dean. I don't need any more time." She looked around them. The lobby wasn't crowded this time of night, but there were still people milling around. She pushed herself to her feet and prayed they would hold her. "Let's go back to the room and talk."

"Talk, huh? That doesn't sound good." He took her hand and they walked in silence down the hushed hallway to their room.

Once the door was closed behind them, Sarah turned and looked at Dean. What a wonderful man he was. So much more than the rebel stereotype she had the crush on years ago.

This was a man who gave her adventure simply because she asked. This was a man who bought silly bookmarks at a fair to make someone feel better. A man who taught her how to play pool, cook hot dogs, and make love in a sleeping bag. She would miss him every morning when she woke up and every evening when she went to bed.

She didn't blame him for not telling her the truth. She'd made no secret of the fact that she wanted an adventure. That she wanted him to be the bad boy he used to be. The biker she could rebel with.

Besides, she hadn't been truthful with him either.

"I'm so sorry, Dean, but I don't love you." The lie burned her tongue like the acid churning in her stomach, but she couldn't think of any other way to set him free. She turned away from him so she didn't have to see the anguish she put on his face. The rest of her speech came out in a rush, before she could take it back.

"You were right when you said I wanted you to be the reckless rebel, the love 'em and leave 'em guy I remembered. I just wanted an exciting fling, Dean. I thought I made that clear. I'm flattered by your proposal, but I don't want to get married. I...I don't want to have children." She steeled herself and turned back around to face him. "But if you ever come back to Buffalo again, I'd love another ride on the Harley."

The distress on Dean's face instantly vanished and his expression turned to stone. He shook his head. "I was wrong about you." His gaze burned her as he slowly scanned her body. "You sure had me fooled. You played the good girl a little too well."

"And you played the bad boy perfectly."

He nodded. "I guess neither one of us was entirely honest."

"I'm sorry, Dean."

"Yeah."

They stood there in the center of the impersonal hotel room, staring at each other. Sarah could think of no words that could make this situation any better, but she struggled to find some.

Finally, she gave up.

She sighed and turned away. "I'm tired." She stripped her dress off and left it lying on the floor. The breeze from the air conditioning left goose bumps on her skin and made her shiver. Or was it the thought of never seeing Dean again? She didn't want to think about it anymore and crawled under the covers at the edge of the king-sized bed.

The bed they never did get to make love in.

She caught her breath when the mattress sagged and Dean crawled in beside her. She shouldn't have been surprised. There was no sofa in the hotel room. Where did she expect him to sleep? She clasped her arms to her chest so they wouldn't automatically reach out and pull him into her arms.

As exhausted as she was, Sarah lay awake most of the night. The what ifs and if onlys kept running through her mind. And the rest of the time, she was so conscious of Dean she could hardly bear it. He was lying close to her, yet he was so far away. The scent of him tempted her, the warmth of his body teased. She clung to the edge of the bed, making sure not to get close enough to touch him.

She matched him breath by uneven breath, all night long.

The silence pulsed around them as they got ready to leave in the morning. Sarah took a quick shower, trying not to remember the feel of Dean's hands on her body under the make-believe waterfall the night before.

While Dean was in the bathroom, she took a few moments to catch up on her journal. Her fingers fumbled with the pen as her brain struggled with the words to describe the last few days. She knew now, though, that she wouldn't need her words

167

scribbled on paper to remember this trip.

Every moment would be etched on her heart forever.

For the first time in his life, Dean wished he wasn't traveling on his bike. They needed a car. A big car. Even though Sarah wasn't holding onto him like she did when they first started out, he could still sense her on the seat behind him. He swore he could even detect her scent in the air around him.

She would haunt him for the rest of his life.

He wasn't going to beg her to reconsider. She was old enough to know her own mind, her own heart. He wasn't going to hang around where he wasn't wanted, that was for sure.

But damn, he was going to miss her. Miss the sunshine she spread around her every day. The way she made him laugh. The feel of her skin next to his.

And he'd miss the life he thought he would have with her.

He was relieved when they finally made Denver. He'd phoned ahead so Terry would know they were coming. She was out the door, her long dark hair flying behind her, as soon as they pulled in the drive.

"You made it!" she cried.

And ran to Sarah.

Sarah climbed stiffly off the bike and stood a moment, as if testing her legs on solid ground. Motorcycle riding had been hard on Sarah. Oh well, she wouldn't have to worry about it anymore.

He stood alone and watched as she and Terry embraced. Then he heard the door slam and Mike and Zach, Terry's two little boys, ran up to Dean.

"Hi, Uncle Dean!" Mikey called out. "Can we sit on the bike?" Zach, always shadowing his older brother, nodded in agreement.

"Sure," Dean said. He lifted the boys up onto the seat, keeping watch on Sarah out of the corner of his eye. She was walking up and down the sidewalk a little ways, like she was trying to stretch out her legs. She shook her hands out again, like she sometimes did. Maybe she had a pinched nerve that made her hands go to sleep. Maybe he'd mention it to her.

Maybe he should mind his own business.

"Hey, Unca Dean," Zach called. "Look at me!" Dean dragged his attention away from Sarah and back to his nephews where it belonged. Zach had grabbed the handlebars and hiked himself as far as he could up the fuel tank.

"Take it easy, Bud," Dean said. "Don't want you falling off the Harley. Your Mom would yell at me."

Zach laughed and Mikey joined in. Dean grabbed one little boy under each arm and swung them off the bike.

Terry finally turned to him. "Hey, guy. Did you have a good trip?"

"Except for a killer thunderstorm, yeah."

"Well, I fixed supper for everyone tonight. I knew you'd be bushed." More often that not, Terry took pity on Dean and invited him for supper.

Now Terry looked back and forth between Dean and Sarah, as if she were studying them. She grinned. "You both look awful. You should have gotten some more sleep."

Her light-hearted comment wouldn't have hurt a day ago, but now the pain sliced through Dean. He caught Sarah's gaze and saw the same pain reflected there. Without a word, she turned away from him and followed Terry into the house.

Terry's husband, Joe, got home from work a few minutes later. He asked Dean about the trip and came up with enough questions to distract Dean until Terry called them in for supper.

Terry had set up the meal in the seldom-used dining room. Candles and flowers in the center of the table were special touches he knew she used to show them how pleased she was that they were there. Dean was so glad that Terry had been able to escape their past and make herself a wonderful family. A loving home.

It should have given him hope that, someday, he would be able to do that too. But without Sarah, he didn't care anymore.

"So what was your favorite part of the trip, Sarah?" Terry asked after all the food had been dished up.

Sarah's eyes flicked briefly to Dean's. "Um, riding the bike, I guess. I'd never done that before."

"Even though it hurts you when you get off?" Dean asked.

"It doesn't hurt," she said quickly. He noticed she fumbled with her fork. She must have been surprised he actually spoke to her after the day they'd had so far. "I'm just a little stiff after riding all day."

"Uncle Dean's not 'tiff," Mikey piped in.

"Yeah, well, I ride a lot."

"Going in the biker bar was fun too," Sarah added.

"You took her to a biker bar?" Terry asked.

Dean laughed at the horrified tone of her voice. "Don't yell at me. She's the one who wanted to go."

Sarah smiled, a bit sadly, but Dean knew he was probably the only one who would notice. "Hey, I learned how to play pool and drink beer."

"Great," Terry said sarcastically, glancing at her two sons. "You're a terrific influence, Dean."

"Oh, but he was," Sarah said quickly. "He was great. He was just what I needed at the time."

At the time.

Not all the time. Not for the rest of her life. She only needed him to provide an adventure for her. And now she assumed the adventure was all over. Didn't she realize the rest of her life could be the greatest adventure of all?

But if she didn't love him, it wasn't up to him to provide her excitement any longer.

He still couldn't stop watching her. His fingers itched to tangle themselves in the silky strands of her hair and trail down the soft skin on her neck. He longed to kiss her throat, right there where her pulse beat wildly when they were making love.

Sarah must have been exhausted. She pushed the food around on her plate and dropped her fork more than once. There were dark circles under her eyes that he'd never noticed before. She must not have slept any better than he did last night. What a sad ending to their trip that they spent their first night in a bed together doing everything in their power not to touch each other.

But if she didn't love him, he had to stop thinking about making love to her. Had to stop wanting to pull her into his arms and kiss her senseless. Had to stop thinking about a family, because he couldn't imagine ever finding anyone who would come close to what Sarah was to him.

He watched Sarah limp into the kitchen to help Terry with the dishes. He roughhoused with his nephews for a few minutes, and then left them watching TV with their dad while he was reluctantly drawn back to Sarah like that proverbial moth to the flame.

Dean was headed down the hallway from the living room to the kitchen when he heard his sister saying something to Sarah. It was the concern he heard in her voice that brought him up short.

"...I'm only asking because I care about you," Terry was saying.

"I know," Sarah replied. "But really, I'm okay. Just very tired. I didn't sleep well last night."

"Can I ask you something else?"

Sarah hesitated for a moment, then he heard her say, "Sure."

"Did you have that limp before you took off on this motorcycle trip?"

Dean took a silent step closer to the doorway to the kitchen. He was dying to look at Sarah, but he had the feeling she might be more forthcoming with Terry if she didn't know he was listening.

"Um, well, a little," Sarah replied. "It's not that bad. Dean gave me a massage one night. That was nice." Dean could hear the forced levity in her voice.

"How about the clumsiness? The problems with your balance?" Terry asked, her voice smooth and calm, like the tone Dean tried to use when he was talking to his clients. "And I noticed you shaking your hands tonight. Do you have numbness in your fingers?"

When Terry listed all those symptoms like that, it sounded serious. Why hadn't he ever put it all together? He'd just explained each of those symptoms away separately, never dreaming they were related.

"Terry," Sarah said. Dean heard the legs of a chair scrape against the floor. She'd probably stood up. Ready to run. "Really, don't worry about me."

"Sarah, I'm talking as a friend here. I think you should consider seeing a neurologist. I work for one, and your symptoms just make me nervous. A neurologist is a doctor that deals with..."

"I know what a neurologist is," Sarah snapped. "I have seen a neuro. More than one. I've had a hundred tests and then a million more."

Dean held his breath and his body started to shake. What was she saying? What did she mean?

"Oh, honey," he heard Terry say. "What was the diagnosis?"

"MS."

MS? Random thoughts flashed through Dean's brain like strobe lights. MS? Was that what Jerry Lewis did the telethon for every year? No, that was muscular dystrophy. What was MS? Oh, yeah, multiple sclerosis. He'd bet it could cause all those symptoms Terry listed.

Pictures started flashing now. Sarah limping. Dropping things. Falling in front of a moving truck.

"Sarah!" The roar was out of Dean's mouth an instant before he burst into the kitchen.

Sarah backed away from his outburst. She stumbled against a chair and nearly fell, catching herself on the counter.

Terry rushed over to Sarah. "Are you all right?" After Sarah nodded, Terry glared at Dean. "Calm down."

His heart was pounding so hard his chest hurt. "Not possible."

He stared at Sarah. At least she had the decency to look guilty.

Terry looked from Dean to Sarah and back again. "Okay, but don't yell at her anymore. She's been through enough. I'm going to go into the living room with the guys. Sarah, if you want to talk later, I'll be here for you."

Sarah nodded again. After Terry left, she turned back to Dean, her chin held high.

How could he have ever thought he knew her? He felt as if he was staring at a stranger. "You have MS? That's why you've been limping? Why you've been falling? You let me believe it was from riding the bike."

"I didn't want to tell you."

"You didn't think I deserved to know?"

"I didn't think it was necessary."

That hurt more than hearing her say she didn't love him. "Not necessary. I see. That's right, I was only good for giving you a little excitement. A little sex. Your own personal adventure. I wasn't worth letting into your life."

"I didn't want your pity, all right?" she cried out. "I didn't want you treating me differently. I just wanted to have this one good time before I went home and watched the rest of my life go by."

"What are you talking about?"

"Dean, MS is a progressive disease. I'm going to get worse. There's a good chance I could end up in a wheelchair. I might not be able to hold a fork or a toothbrush."

"Sarah..." This was all happening too fast. He didn't know what to think. What to say or do.

"I'm not the wife you want. If we had children, they'd be ashamed of a mother who is different. Other kids would laugh because I stumble and fall down." She stared at Dean, probably to make sure he got the message.

He did. "This is different than my father and you know it."

"The cause may be different, but the embarrassment for our children would be the same." She reached out for the chair and held on as she lowered herself down onto the seat. "I'm never getting married or having children. And I'm certainly not burdening any man with a future spent taking care of me."

Drive the stake deeper. "Any man? Am I just any man?"

"No, of course not. You're an active man with a future full of traveling and raising children and riding bikes. That's not my future, Dean."

Dean started to pace around the small kitchen. Too many thoughts were whirling through his head. Too many emotions fighting for room inside him. He had to sort things out. He had to get out of there to do it.

He stuck his head out into the hallway. "Terry! Can Sarah stay here tonight?"

"Uh, sure?" The question was in her voice, but she didn't ask him why.

He turned to Sarah. She looked so small and helpless in that chair. In fact, she looked scared to death. He wanted to drag her into his arms and soothe her fears, but there was nothing he could do unless she could conquer them herself.

"I guess you're right. We don't have any future together." She nodded, her face pale, her eyes bright with unshed tears. He hardened himself against feeling sorry for her. "Yeah, it takes courage to plan for the future. But you'd rather hide or run away, wouldn't you?"

She stared at him, color flooding back into her face. "What?"

"Yeah, it's just another excuse. First you blamed your parents because you say they expected you to be the good, stay-at-home girl. Now you blame an illness for keeping you from living life."

She lunged to her feet and swayed a little to gain her balance. He had to stop himself from reaching out to catch her. Instead, he turned away from her and crossed the kitchen to the outside door. He looked back and tried to ignore the painful knot in his stomach.

"It's too bad, Sarah. We could have had one hell of an adventure together."

Chapter Twelve

After Dean closed the door behind him, Sarah heard him take the stairs up to his apartment with slow, heavy steps. Her heart pounded in her chest and her sorrow throbbed in her head. Terry came into the kitchen, her concern evident on her face. "Are you all right?"

Sarah nodded, but didn't meet her eyes. "Can I borrow your Yellow Pages? I need to book a flight back to Buffalo right away."

"Oh, honey. Stay a little longer. Give him some time to get used to the idea."

Maybe Dean was right. Maybe she was a coward. He could call it running away if he wanted to. She certainly didn't want to risk seeing the disappointment in his face. "No, I have to get back."

Terry was quiet for a moment, then she crossed to the sink. "You don't have to go right this minute. How about some herbal tea?"

Sarah started to protest, but then shrugged her shoulders. Why not? She wasn't going anywhere tonight.

She watched Terry heat some water in the microwave and drop tea bags in two cups. Her heartbeat gradually slowed down to normal, but her head still felt like it was going to explode.

"It's chamomile," Terry told her. "It's supposed to be relaxing." She sat down beside Sarah and slid a cup into her shaking hands. "Now. How can you leave? You're in love with my brother."

"I never said I was in love with Dean."

"Honey, you didn't have to say anything. It's written all over your face. It's all over his too."

"I know." Sarah would never forget the wonderful words of love he spoke to her last night. "I never expected that to happen."

"Me, either," Terry said. "I was afraid he'd never get beyond his past."

"What do you mean?"

"Our father made it clear that he expected Dean to turn out to be a bastard like he was. Dean's been fighting that prediction his whole life." Terry set down her tea and flipped her long hair out of her face. "Sarah, he's done so well. Stopped drinking. Graduated college. Got a job he loved." Terry sighed. "But he never lasted with any woman for very long. I think he kept his heart out of relationships on purpose, whether they were businesswomen or bimbos."

"Terry, I don't need to hear all this..."

She went on as if Sarah had never spoken. "I'm thrilled that he's willing to even think about being a husband and a father. I know he was so afraid our father would be right. I guess all Dean had to do was to find the right woman."

Sarah stared into the tea cup. She remembered how natural he'd looked playing with Terry's sons. He'd make a wonderful father. If only...no, she wasn't going there.

"I'm not the right woman for him."

"He seems to think so."

Not anymore.

"He's wrong. That's why I need to leave as soon as I can. So Dean can get on with the rest of his life."

"And what about you?"

"I'll get on with the rest of mine." And try to be satisfied with the memories.

"You know that the majority of people with MS can live relatively normal lives."

"I also know that no one can tell how far the illness will progress," Sarah replied. "Remember Mrs. Cheney?"

"Oh, Sarah, there's no reason to think you'll be like Mrs. Cheney. Besides, there's all sorts of new medications out there now that weren't available back when we were in grade school."

"But no one can say for sure. I don't want that kind of uncertain future for Dean."

"Isn't that up to him to decide?" Terry asked. "I see lots of people with MS. Yes, there are problems, but you learn to adjust. You'll both learn to adjust."

She wouldn't let Terry's arguments sway her. She wouldn't give in to the temptation to believe it could possibly work out. "Just get me the phone book, please. Don't make this any harder than it already is."

Terry turned, opened a drawer, and pulled out the phone book. She handed it to Sarah, but didn't let go when Sarah reached for it. Terry's eyes bore into hers.

"Where are your meds?"

Sarah sighed. "They're on order. I was only just diagnosed."

"Oh, hon, then you haven't even given yourself time to get used to this yet, much less Dean. Don't run off before giving both of you time to come to terms with this."

"I'm not running off," Sarah said. "I'm going home." But

Dean's accusations rang in her ears.

Terry let go of the phone book. "Fine. Leave the man who loves you. The man you love. Go back to Buffalo."

Back to Buffalo. Back to her old life. The safe, sensible life.

Was Dean right? Had she been hiding behind excuses her whole life? Was it easier to make excuses than venture out of her comfort zone? The secure job, the safe apartment?

Had she made up excuses rather than risk failure? Like the time she tried out for a part in the school play, forgot her lines and everyone laughed at her. She never put herself in that position again.

Was she making excuses now? Was she refusing Dean's proposal for his sake? Or for her own?

Because when it came right down to it, Dean hadn't known about the MS when he asked her to marry him. She was so afraid when he found out what was involved in her illness, he'd walk away anyway.

Was she protecting him? Or protecting her heart?

Terry set Sarah up in their computer room. Sarah closed the door and sank down onto the sofa bed. The hollow ache that had started in her stomach seemed to have spread through her whole body.

How could she live the rest of her life without Dean? Without his quiet strength? His dynamite kisses? With only the memory of these few days and nights for comfort?

Enough whining. It was what it was.

She pulled the cell phone out of her waist pack. She had to stop thinking about the glide of Dean's fingers along her skin. Now was not the time to remember the night they had created their own sparks during that thunderstorm. She had to stop thinking about how empty her life was going to be without Dean to bring her the adventure.

It was time to get back to the real world.

She had to start planning the rest of her life. She supposed she could work at the bank for as long as she was able to handle the money without fumbling too badly. She'd have to look for a ground floor apartment before her balance deteriorated. And she'd need a new car to replace the one that died of old age.

Maybe she'd plan a trip to Florida to see her sister. Maybe she could do that without letting the excuses stop her. It was a place to start.

She fumbled with the keypad on her cell phone and dialed her mother. She was surprised at the relief she felt when her mother answered. "Mom?"

"Are you all right?" her mother asked. "Where are you?"

"I'm fine. I'm in Denver. At Terry's house. I'm flying out tomorrow morning. Can you pick me up at the airport?"

"Of course. Did you have a good time, sweetheart?"

"Yeah." Sarah paused and then asked the question that had been bothering her for hours. "Mom, why did you always expect me to be the sensible one?"

"I don't know what you mean."

"For heaven's sake, you and Dad called me Sensible Sarah, like it was my full name," she cried. "I couldn't do anything. I had to set the example for my younger sisters. Why did you do that to me?"

"Do *what* to you?" her mother asked sharply. "Sarah, what are you talking about?"

"You didn't let me do anything. I had to be the good girl. I didn't want to disappoint you."

"Oh, honey. I never knew you felt that way. It's not that we expected you to be sensible. That's the way you were."

Now it was Sarah's turn to ask, "What do you mean?"

"Even as a little child you were always so careful. So cautious. Like when you started to walk and you fell down? You didn't get up and try again. Not right away like your sisters did." Her mother paused, and she cleared her throat. "Now maybe as new parents your father and I were a little too protective of you. We may have told you to be careful more often because you were our first.

"But you never liked to take risks, Sarah. I don't think your father or I had anything to do with that. You were sensible all on your own, Sarah. That's how you got that name."

"I never knew that," Sarah told her. "Sometimes, you know, it just seemed like such a heavy burden."

Or was it a convenient excuse?

There was a knock at the door. Sarah told her mother what time to pick her up at the airport and disconnected. She pulled herself up from the sofa, her legs heavy, her body exhausted. When she opened the door, she found Dean on the other side.

He wasn't much more than a dark shadow looming over her in the dim hallway. He was breathing heavily, as if he'd just run around the block. As if he'd just been making wild, passionate love. Or as if he was really, really angry.

She stepped back and he followed her into the room, closing the door behind him.

"I could strangle you," he said, his voice rough and strained. She could tell he was holding his anger on a tight rein.

"Dean…"

"Don't talk to me right now. Do you know what I've been doing for the past few hours?"

She shook her head. Her body shook and it had nothing to do with the MS.

"I've been on the Internet. Researching multiple sclerosis. And I talked to Terry." He started pacing back and forth in front of her. He sounded as if he were speaking through clenched teeth. "Did you know that the majority of people with MS never need a wheelchair? Never." He stopped in front of her. "Did you know that heat makes the symptoms worse?"

She remembered feeling better after being in the air-conditioned laundry room. "I kinda figured that out."

"You should have told me, Sarah! Did you know that being tired makes your symptoms worse? I endangered your life by riding all day and not stopping so you could rest! No wonder you fell in front of that truck. You could have been killed and it would have been my fault."

"None of it was your fault."

"You should have told me, Sarah."

"I didn't think it would matter. I didn't think anything would happen." It was time for her to be truthful now. "You see, I only found out last week. I didn't want it to be true. I'd been feeling better lately. I honestly didn't think I would have any symptoms on this trip." She dropped down onto the sofa. "I was running away, Dean. If I admitted it to you, I would have had to admit it to myself."

Dean sank down onto the sofa beside her. His anger seemed to have drained away. "The trip could have been so different. We could have stopped during the hottest part of the day and you could have rested. I blame myself for not catching on. I thought your limp was from riding on the bike. It wasn't, was it?"

"No. I'm sorry, Dean. I know now I should have told you, but after I started having problems, I still didn't want you to know. I didn't want you to feel sorry for me. I didn't want you treating me differently because of it." She paused, and finally admitted her real fear. "And I didn't want the adventure to end."

"What do you mean? End?"

"I was afraid once you knew about my illness, you'd send me home. I was afraid you wouldn't have let me go with you to begin with if you'd known."

"I wouldn't have sent you home, Sarah."

She shrugged. "We'll never know for sure, will we? I'm sorry I ruined what we had together."

"It doesn't have to be ruined," Dean said softly. "We can go on from here."

Sarah took a deep breath, but couldn't say the words she knew he wanted to hear. She looked out the window at the fading light.

Dean shifted beside her. "Sarah? Where do we go from here?"

She looked away from the window and back to Dean. "Well, um, I go to the airport in the morning and go back to Buffalo. I'll take a taxi, you don't have to take me."

"Is that what you want to do?" he asked so softly she could barely hear him.

She refused to shed any more tears. "It's what I have to do."

"You don't have to go back," he said, the hope ringing clearly in his voice. "You can stay here with me. You can marry me."

"I can't."

He surged to his feet and stepped away from her. "That's right. You don't love me, do you?"

She had to swallow twice before she could get the words out. "I'm...I'm sorry, Dean."

"I'm sorry too." He turned and walked out the door without another glance her way.

After tossing and turning for what seemed like forever, Sarah finally gave up on sleep. One look out the window at the night sky and she dragged the light blanket off the mattress as she crawled out of bed. She managed to quietly limp down the hall and out the back door.

There was an old glider on the back porch and she curled up in a corner, wrapping the blanket around her like a shawl. Slowly gliding back and forth, she looked up into the star-speckled sky and tried not to think about the flight she'd booked for the next morning.

She'd never gotten her chance to sleep under the stars. She would miss camping. Miss seeing the world fly by on the back of a Harley.

Let's face it, she would miss Dean.

Was she really the coward Dean accused her of being? After all, she'd gotten the adventure she had wanted. She'd even gotten the awesome love affair to remember. She'd never have experienced those things if she hadn't dared to talk Dean into this trip in the first place.

As she sat back and watched the sky, a wispy cloud drifted across the moon. A pair of headlights swept across the horizon in front of her and she wondered where the car was going so late at night. An occasional bird silently glided by in the moonlight.

So where did that leave her now? She wrapped the blanket a little more tightly around her shoulders to ward off a chill that had nothing to do with the cool night air.

The adventure was over. So was the affair. She was left sitting on the porch in the middle of the night, dreaming of being in Dean's arms again.

Sarah shot upright as she realized she was living her worst nightmare right now, already sitting on a porch, watching life go by.

Why had she given up so easily? Why had she let excuses rule her life? She may have been Sensible Sarah once, but that didn't mean she had to stay that way.

She looked over at the shadowy stretch of stairs that led upstairs from the end of the porch. They were the only thing besides herself standing between her and Dean. She rose to her feet, leaving the blanket on the glider. The stars winked at her, ridiculously, like they were trying to give her hope.

She shook her hands out once before she grasped the railing. She took a deep breath and took the first step. She clutched the railings hard with hands that tingled with pins and needles. She didn't look up to see how long the flight of stairs was, but concentrated on taking them one at a time, dragging up her weak foot when she needed to. The thought of reaching Dean kept her going.

Halfway up the stairs, her stubborn foot slipped. She cried out as her knee landed on the step. She was able to keep her grip on the railing, however, and not fall any farther. After a deep breath and a curse under her breath, she resumed her climb.

What should have been a quick trot seemed to take forever, but she made it to the top.

He was waiting for her there. He put his arms around her when she reached the landing. "What are you doing here?"

She was breathing heavily. The climb had taken more out of her than she thought. But she felt great, just the same.

"Of course, you have to live at the top of one of the longest, steepest sets of stairs I've ever seen in my life."

He chuckled. "Of course."

"I had to come. Had to tell you I'm sorry. I handled everything so badly." She turned and grasped his hand. "But I love you," she went on, before anything could stop her from saying it. "I do. I lied when I said I didn't."

"I know." He kissed the top of her head and put his arm around her. It felt so right. "Come on inside."

When they were settled on the soft, leather sofa in his living room, Dean asked, "Why did you lie to me?"

"I was afraid. Afraid of what your life would be like if you're saddled with me..."

"Whoa, saddled with you? Where do you get that?"

"No matter how you look at it, there's a very real chance that I will end up being a burden to you. You don't want that kind of future."

"I want the kind of future that has you in it." He took her hand and squeezed it lightly. "Did you think you were going to scare me off?"

She chewed on her bottom lip and nodded.

"Well, that worked for about two seconds. I'm not afraid to take a chance on what the future holds. Don't you know that life itself is the real adventure? You have to take what comes along and make the best of it."

"But what if I do end up in a wheelchair?"

"Remember that woman you met in the laundry room at that campground?"

"Yes, I remember her."

"Did you meet her husband?"

"No."

"I did. At the camp store. Did you know he's in a

wheelchair?"

"He is? She never mentioned it." Could it be that it just wasn't that big a deal to them? "And they travel in their RV all year long?"

"People in wheelchairs can do all kinds of things. You don't have to use it as an excuse."

"But what if..."

"Sarah, I could crash my Harley and end up in a wheelchair someday, but I'm not going to give up riding my bike." Suddenly, he shot to his feet. "Yes, I will. If that's what it takes to convince you, I will sell my bike and never ride again."

"Dean, no!"

"But, you know, I could be in a car accident just as easily. I'd better get rid of my winter car and walk to work. Of course, then, do you know how many pedestrians get hit by a vehicle every year? Nope, I guess I'd better just sit home and do nothing. But that wouldn't even guarantee that I wouldn't get hurt. Do you know how many people slip and fall in their own bathtubs every day? Maybe I should stop taking showers too."

Sarah couldn't help but laugh. "No, I don't think you have to go that far."

He sat down beside her and took her hands. "You and I can't guarantee that life will be perfect. No one has that guarantee. We take the good with the bad and live our lives the best we can. But we have to be willing to take the risk. No excuses."

No excuses. The possibility both excited her and scared her to death. She'd depended on them for a long time. Could she throw all her excuses away and dare to live life to the fullest?

He squeezed her hands. "So what do you say?"

Did she dare risk it all? Her heart? Her life? Her future?

"Life is too precious to waste a minute of it," Dean said, gathering her into his arms. "I don't want to spend the rest of my life alone. Do you?"

Suddenly her future opened up before her, bright with possibilities. She placed her palm against his cheek and savored the feel of him. She realized that she could actually keep what she wanted to have.

"I love you," she said. "Will you ever get tired of hearing that?"

"Never," he said. "So, what do you say about our future?"

"Hmm, let's see. A future with love and laughter and adventure. And you." She pressed her lips to his and the warmth radiating from the man she loved banished the chill that had penetrated deep in her bones. She couldn't think of a single excuse.

She looked around them, an unexpected thrill running through her. She ran her hand over his arm, touching him as she was afraid she would never do again. "Do you have a bed around here? A real bed?"

Dean grinned. "Of course."

"Well, I think it is only fair that I get to make love in a real bed with the man I'm going to marry."

Dean stood up and, without warning, swept her up into his arms. He captured her lips with his, mingling his breath with hers, sealing their promise to each other. "A sensible woman. I like that."

Epilogue

Dean knew the nurse thought she should be the one to push the wheelchair, but there was no way he was trusting the welfare of its precious cargo to anyone else. He smiled down at Sarah and tried not to laugh at her sputtering.

As he pushed the wheelchair down the hospital hallway he could hardly believe it had been five years since he and Sarah had made that fateful trip on his Harley. He didn't want to think about what his life would have been like if he hadn't given into her blatant blackmail.

He leaned down and kissed her ear. "Don't worry, we're almost there."

"I know, I just..." Sarah stopped talking when a little boy with blond hair and big eyes came running up the hallway toward them.

"Mommy! Daddy!" he cried.

Dean let go of the wheelchair and knelt down, scooping Jason up into his arms. He decided he could allow the nurse to wheel the chair the final few feet down to the lobby. "Jason, you were supposed to stay with Grandma."

"Yeah, 'til you comed down. And you did."

As they reached the lobby, Jason wriggled out of Dean's arms.

"Gramma. Gramma," Jason called out. He ran to Sarah's mother, grabbed her hand, and brought her over to the wheelchair. "I'm a big brother now. This is my baby sister. We gotta take good care of her 'cuz she's so little."

"She's beautiful," Reva said, looking down at the little pink bundle in Sarah's arms. Her eyes teared up as she looked at Sarah and Dean.

He lucked out when he married Sarah. Not only did he get an incredible woman for his wife, but when Reva moved out to Colorado after Jason was born, Dean got a wonderful woman for a mother.

He knelt beside Sarah and sweet little Lily, and put his arm around Jason. His family. Dean found his eyes tearing up as well. He didn't know how caring for a wife and children could come so naturally with the upbringing he'd had, but Dean didn't question it.

He thanked God every night for bringing Sarah into his life.

"Hey, can I get out of this thing?" Sarah asked. Without waiting for a reply, she stood up and stepped away from the wheelchair. "I may be a little sore, but I can still get around under my own power."

"I brought the van around front," Reva said. "Do you want me to take Jason home with me until you get settled in?"

"Nice try, Mom. But we're in this together, aren't we guys?" She turned and smiled at Dean and their son.

"Yeah. We're a team," Jason said.

"You bet we are. I can't wait to get home. I want to get this sweetie settled in and spend some time with my guys."

Dean held onto Jason's hand and put his other arm around Sarah. She limped only slightly as they headed for the minivan they bought after they'd discovered Jason was on the way.

Sarah was doing so well. The medications she took worked wonders in slowing the progression of the MS.

They stepped out into the bright sunshine. A cool autumn breeze swept around them. Sarah flipped the blanket over the baby's head.

When they reached the van, Reva said, "I made a casserole for you for dinner. I'll drop it by later."

"Thanks, Mom. Make it much later, okay? I think the four of us are going to take a nap when we get home."

Reva laughed. "Call me when you get up."

Dean took the baby from Sarah and helped her ease herself into the passenger seat of the van. Before he shut the door, he leaned over and kissed the mother of his children, the woman who made his life complete. The one who still made his blood pound and his body harden.

Whoa, boy, no sense thinking about that. It was going to be a little while before they could do anything more than sleep together, and with a new baby in the house again, he knew they wouldn't even get that much sleep.

"How was I ever lucky enough to get you?"

She smiled up at him. "I guess we were meant to be together."

The tiny bundle in his arms squirmed and Dean's heart swelled with joy. "Meant to be together, huh? You can't come up anything better than that?"

"Why? You don't think that's a sensible answer?"

Dean laughed. "Sensible? Since when were you ever sensible?"

"You're right," she said, and beamed him the smile he would never tire of. "I've never been sensible as far as you're concerned."

Dean kissed her again. Jason climbed into his car seat and Dean placed Lily in the new one beside her big brother. He buckled them both safely in.

Lily opened her eyes as he was fastening the last strap. Dean smiled at the precious little person that was a part of him and Sarah. "Hey, little girl. Welcome to your life. Are you ready for a great adventure?"

He could have sworn she nodded her head.

Sarah laughed. "Come on, Daddy. Let's get our little ones home."

Dean climbed in the van beside her and kissed her once again. "It keeps getting better and better, doesn't it?

"Every day," she said. "The adventure gets better every day."

About the Author

To learn more about Natasha Moore, please visit www.natashamoore.com. Send an email to Natasha Moore at natasha@natashamoore.com or join her Yahoo! group to join in the fun with other readers as well as Natasha Moore! http://groups.yahoo.com/group/natashamoore

When a dangerous stalker shakes her world, can Sallie trust
Cade enough to reveal her secret past?

Cade's Challenge
© *2007 Becky Barker*

Someone is stalking Sallie Archer, and Cade Langden is determined to find out who. When the stalker turns his attentions toward the company Cade built from a dream and a design on a napkin, things get really personal.

After years of working together in perfect harmony, faced with this new threat, Cade and Sallie realize that, no matter how much she wants to keep things strictly business, the chemistry between them is too strong to ignore.

But Sallie is keeping a secret and the truth about her past could destroy any chance of a future...

Available now in ebook and print from Samhain Publishing.

"I guess I could drink another beer."

Cade laughed, a deep husky sound that reverberated between them. "So you like the beer?" he asked, motioning for the waitress to bring them two more bottles.

"It's pretty disgusting, actually," she declared, scrunching her nose in distaste. "But I've heard it's an acquired taste."

"How many do you figure you have to drink to acquire it?"

"Too many to make the effort, I'm sure," she decided. "But I guess I can sip another one for a while."

"Nurse."

"Pardon?"

"You don't sip a beer, your nurse it."

"We're talking beer-drinker's lingo?"

"Yeah."

"Okay," Sallie conceded. "I can nurse it."

"That's the spirit. You need to lighten up a little."

She gave his casual remark serious consideration. "Why do you say that?"

"I don't know," he said. "It just seems like you need some fun in your life."

"Fun?" She wasn't certain that anything she'd done in her adult life could be called fun. Even as a child, her activities had been carefully orchestrated. She enjoyed a variety of hobbies now, but didn't think he'd qualify any of them as fun.

"Just plain fun," Cade explained in an exasperated tone. "Things like playing ball, shooting pool, horseback riding or skinny dipping. Especially the skinny dipping," he added with a wicked gleam in his eyes.

The mental image his words created made her skin tingle and her nipples tighten. She quickly banished the wayward thoughts. Her eyes flashed with annoyance as they met his over the bottle. She'd die before admitting she'd never done any of those things. It was a pointless conversation, anyway.

He grinned and saluted her with his beer bottle in a blatant attempt to rattle her composure.

"Care to dance?"

Sallie's eyes narrowed at the invitation, and she didn't bother to disguise her mistrust. Cade might seem like a carefree guy to most of the world, but she knew he didn't do anything without serious thought and consideration.

"I don't know how," she declared flatly, and then took a big swallow of beer. She hoped he'd accept the refusal.

He didn't.

"I've seen you dance plenty of times."

"Ballroom stuff. Not what they're doing." She nodded toward the dance floor.

"I'll teach you."

"And what if I don't want to learn?"

"Humor me," he drawled, his expression daring. "We have half an hour or so to wait, and I like to dance."

Sallie glanced around the room, feeling pressured. Surely there was someone else he could ask to dance. There were several other couples doing some sort of line dance on the tiny floor. The number of women in the bar seemed to have increased since she'd entered, yet none of them looked single or in search of a partner.

"You're the only candidate," he insisted, reading her thoughts. "It's not safe to pick up strange partners these days, you know."

"I really don't care to learn whatever they're doing."

"It's the boot-scootin' boogie," he explained. "But we can wait for a slow song."

Sallie studied him thoughtfully. She knew it had been several months since his last relationship disintegrated. He was rarely without someone special in his life, but he didn't have to chase women. They always came willingly. There were several vying for his attention right now.

For some reason, he'd been slow in choosing a new lover. He might be longing for feminine company. She had no intention of becoming a stand-in playmate, but the music was tempting.

"I can probably manage a slow dance," she finally announced.

He amazed her by throwing back his head and roaring with laughter. She frowned, genuinely confused and a little hurt. "Why is that so funny?"

He shook his head in disbelief. "Because it took you so damn long to decide. Have you ever done an impulsive thing in your life? Even under the influence of alcohol? You think too much, and I'm not used to having to beg someone for a dance. You need to unwind a little and get rid of some inhibitions."

It was Sallie's turn to shake her head. "No, thank you." She wanted control of everything around her, always. She might be the most organized schedule-slave he'd ever known, but that didn't bother her a bit.

When a deep frown replaced Cade's smile, she wondered where his thoughts had drifted. Did he think her need for control was boring and cowardly? She'd outgrown the adolescent desire to be daring, uninhibited and adventurous. The price for that sort of lifestyle was way too high.

For a couple of minutes they were both quiet while they finished their beers and studied each other more intently. Sallie wondered what the greater risk would be, meeting with an anonymous snitch or letting the boss take her in his arms again.

GREAT cheap fun

Discover eBooks!

THE FASTEST WAY TO GET THE HOTTEST NAMES

Get your favorite authors on your favorite reader, long before they're out in print! Ebooks from Samhain go wherever you go, and work with whatever you carry—Palm, PDF, Mobi, and more.

Samhain Publishing Ltd

WWW.SAMHAINPUBLISHING.COM

Printed in the United States
126221LV00004B/139-150/P